Matr

MW01134687

Cozy Mystery Series Book Eleven

Hope Callaghan

hopecallaghan.com
Copyright © 2018
All rights reserved.

*****

Visit my website for new releases and special offers: hopecallaghan.com

Thank you to these wonderful ladies who help make my books shine - Peggy H., Cindi G., Jean P., Wanda D., Barbara W. and Renate P. for taking the time to preview *Matrimony & Mayhem,* for the extra sets of eyes and for catching all of my mistakes.

A special THANKS to my reader review team:

Alice, Amary, Barbara, Becky, Brinda, Cassie, Charlene, Christina, Deb, Debbie, Dee, Denota, Devan, Diana, Diann, Grace, Helen, Jan, Jo-Ann, Joyce, Jean K., Jean M., Katherine, Lynne, Megan, Melda, Kat, Linda, Lynne, Pat, Patsy, Paula, Rebecca, Rita, Tamara, Valerie, Vicki and Virginia.

CONTENTS

Cast of Characters

Carlita Garlucci. The widow of a mafia "made" man, Carlita promised her husband on his deathbed to get their sons out of the "family" business, so she moves from New York to the historic city of Savannah, Georgia. But escaping the family isn't as easy as she hoped it would be and trouble follows Carlita to her new home.

Mercedes Garlucci. Carlita's daughter and the first to move to Savannah with her mother. An aspiring writer, Mercedes has a knack for finding mysteries and adventure.

Vincent Garlucci, Jr. Carlita's oldest son and a younger version of his father, Vinnie is deeply entrenched in the "family business" and is not interested in leaving New York.

Tony Garlucci. Carlita's middle son and the first to follow his mother to Savannah. Tony is protective of both his mother and his sister, which is a good thing since the Garlucci women are always in some sort of a predicament.

Paulie Garlucci. Carlita's youngest son. Mayor of the small town of Clifton Falls, NY, Paulie never joined the "family business," and is content to live his life with his wife and young children far away from a life of crime. Gina, Paulie's wife, rules the family household with an iron fist.

Chapter 1

Carlita Garlucci watched the Savannah trolley roll to a stop. She shifted the garment bag to her other arm and reached for the railing. "You're a sight for sore eyes."

"I've been keeping an eye out for you." Claryce Magillicuddy waited for Carlita to board the trolley and swipe her rider card. "I saved the seat behind me, so you wouldn't have to carry all your stuff to the back."

"Thanks, Claryce."

"Reese," her friend corrected.

Carlita's friend recently informed her that she preferred the nickname *Reese* instead of Claryce, deeming her given name as too formal for a Savannah trolley driver. Plus, the riders never could pronounce it correctly, calling her "Claire-ice." Not "Claire-eese."

"Reese." Carlita wiggled onto the seat before draping the garment bag over the back. "I'll be glad when Tony and Shelby are finally hitched. I'm whupped."

"How's your soon-to-be daughter-in-law feeling?" Reese closed the door and shifted the trolley into gear.

"She's finally decided to cut back on her overtime hours at the post office." Shelby had been hard at work planning the wedding, to be held at Ravello's Ristorante, the Garlucci family's new restaurant.

Carlita suspected she was trying to do too much, including volunteering for the extra overtime and complained of being exhausted. During the last few weeks, she had come straight home from work and gone right to bed.

The family was pitching in to keep an eye on Violet while her mom rested, but Carlita was growing increasingly concerned there was something else going on. She'd even gone as far as to ask Tony if Shelby might be pregnant, to which her son adamantly insisted was not the case.

He'd all but told his mother to butt out of their business.

Never one to back down, Carlita finally convinced her son that Shelby needed to see her doctor. "I finally talked some sense into Tony. Shelby has an appointment scheduled for a full check-up right after the wedding."

"Good," Reese said. "I think you're gonna need a vacation."

"If only I could. I'm still working out the kinks at the restaurant. At least I finally found a manager. He came highly recommended by Mike Russo, President of the Savannah Area Restaurant Association." Carlita pushed a wayward strand of hair out of her eyes. "As soon as this wedding is over, I'll be able to get all of my businesses back on track."

"Let me know if there's anything I can do to help." Reese eased alongside the curb to let a group of passengers off while more riders boarded. "Step right up. Welcome to the Big Peach."

Reese's nickname for her pale peach-colored trolley never failed to get a laugh or chuckle from the riders. Even the sourpusses would crack a smile when they spied the giant smiling peach she'd painted on the ceiling of the trolley.

Carlita was one of the first to see Reese's masterpiece. According to her friend, the idea came to her in a dream. "Is your boss going to make you paint over the peach?"

"Nope." Reese's eyes lit. "In fact, the company is considering letting me try my hand at painting the side of their ugly trolley garage. I might have me a small side business in the works."

The trolley turned the corner and rumbled to a stop in front of *Savannah Swag*, the Garlucci family's pawnshop. Carlita stood. "You're still coming to the wedding?"

"I wouldn't miss it for the world. Got my invitation taped to the refrigerator, so I don't forget."

Carlita gathered her belongings and cautiously descended the steps. "I'm sure I'll see you before the wedding, what with half a dozen or more errands yet to run between today and tomorrow."

"You take care of yourself, Carlita. All of the little details will work themselves out one way or another." The doors to the trolley closed and with a quick wave, Reese and the Big Peach were on their way.

Carlita waited until the trolley turned the corner and disappeared from sight before crossing the street and making her way inside the pawnshop.

Tony was in the back, helping a customer. Her daughter, Mercedes, was behind the jewelry counter. She gave her mother a quick nod. "You picked up Tony's suit?"

"Yeah, and we gotta make sure it fits." Carlita zigzagged her way to the employee's area. She hung the suit on a hook near the door and waited for her son to join her.

"You got the goods?"

"Yep. I didn't take a real close look. I figured you better try it on. I'll cover for you."

"Thanks, Ma." Tony lifted the bag. "Shelby left a little while ago. She's on her way to the bakery to check on the wedding cake."

"How is Shelby?"

A somber expression crossed Tony's face. "She's still feeling tired. I'm starting to worry now."

"I would be, too." Carlita had a sudden thought. "You don't think..." Her voice trailed off.

"Think what?"

"You don't think she's getting cold feet?"

"No way. Shelby and I want to get married. We're excited about our new home and Violet is already

6

planning her princess bedroom. We're hopin' it's just because she's got so much goin' on, she's worn herself out."

"Hopefully, it's nothing a few days away, and a honeymoon won't fix."

Tony headed out of the pawnshop. He returned a short time later, looking dapper in his dark suit.

Carlita's breath caught in her throat. "You look so handsome." Her eyes grew damp as she stared at a younger version of her husband, Vinnie.

"No water works." Tony shook his head. "You can't start crying yet."

"But you look so much like your father. I wish he could be here," she whispered.

"I'm sure he's watchin' over us and that he would love Shelby."

Carlita didn't dare speak and only nodded her head.

"I better go change before you start bawlin." Tony backed out of the store and closed the door behind him.

"Hey, Ma." Carlita turned at her daughter's voice.

"Tony got you all choked up?"

"Yes. He looks just like your father."

"Pops would be proud. This is a happy time. No tears." Mercedes squeezed her mother's arm. "Did you get my text?"

"No. You sent me a text?"

"Yeah. Earlier."

Carlita fumbled inside her purse for her cell phone. "I see it now." Her eyes squinted. "Did you need me to pick up something else?"

"No. You've got a surprise," Mercedes said.

"What kind of surprise? Good or bad?"

"I...It could go either way. You'll find out soon enough. It's upstairs, in the apartment."

8

"You bought something for the restaurant," Carlita guessed.

"Nope."

"For the apartment?"

"Nope again." Mercedes shook her head. "Not even close. Like I said, you'll have to wait until you get upstairs."

"Vinnie and Brittney showed up early?"

"Uh-uh. Paulie called earlier. He and the rest of the clan will be here around the same time as Vinnie and Brittney."

The rest of Carlita's children were on their way to Savannah, to help Shelby and Tony celebrate their big day.

The wedding ceremony would take place in the courtyard. Carlita's new restaurant, Ravello's Ristorante, was hosting a reception immediately following the ceremony.

The timing of the wedding was perfect. It would give Carlita an idea how her kitchen and new staff would run before the restaurant opened a few days later.

The guest list was a mix of business associates, immediate family, friends and their close-knit Walton Square neighbors.

The original plan was to invite immediate family only, but as the wedding grew closer, the list grew. It was still manageable, and Carlita was thankful the restaurant was able and ready to host the event.

Ravello's kitchen staff, servers, busboys and greeters were all in place and ready to go. Carlita had done as much as she could to make sure the wedding and the reception went off without a hitch.

"Thanks for picking up the suit, Ma."

"You're welcome. I'm gonna run by the courtyard and then the restaurant before heading to the apartment." Carlita turned to go before turning back. "Will you and Shelby be joining us for dinner?

I'm going all out and ordering Monster Pizza for dinner," she joked.

"We wouldn't miss it."

A customer approached. "Can I have some help over in the gun case?"

"Sure." Tony motioned to his sister. "You tell Ma about her surprise?"

"Not yet." Mercedes smiled slyly.

"I wish I could be there to see the look on her face."

"See what?" A feeling of dread swept over Carlita. "That does it. I'm going upstairs to see my surprise before I do anything else." She marched out the back door and into the hall.

Mercedes hurried after her mother and followed her up the stairs.

"You know how I feel about surprises."

"Wait!" Mercedes sprinted ahead of her mother, blocking the entrance to the apartment. "I have only one thing to say."

"What?"

"For the record, this wasn't my idea." Mercedes opened the door and stepped inside.

Chapter 2

At first glance, Carlita didn't recognize the person standing in front of the balcony doors, his back to her.

"Eddie?"

The man spun around and took a step towards her. "Hey, Carlita. I bet you're surprised to see me."

"Eddie." Carlita repeated herself as she stared at her only sibling, her younger brother, Eddie DelVecchio. "What are you doing here?"

"I'm here for Tony's wedding. I ran into Vito Castellini a coupla weeks ago. He told me his son-in-law and daughter was heading to Savannah for Tony's wedding. I thought I would make a quick trip down here and surprise you."

"Surprise me? More like shock. Where's Anjelica?"

"She's out on your balcony, smoking a cig." Eddie jabbed his thumb toward Carlita's balcony. "I wanted to swing by, check the place out and say 'Hi.' We're not gonna hang around. In fact, we were gettin' ready to head out. We're staying at the swanky new Savannah Riverfront Inn. Nothing but the best for my Anjelica."

"I...had no idea." Carlita pressed the palm of her hand to her forehead. She hadn't seen her brother since Vinnie's funeral a year ago. The siblings were never close, despite the fact that Eddie had been a member of "the family" almost as long as her deceased husband, Vinnie.

The balcony door opened and Anjelica DelVecchio tottered inside, the tip of her stiletto heel catching on the doorframe.

Eddie reached out to steady her. "You're gonna kill yourself in those heels."

"You wish." Anjelica regained her balance, tugging the edge of her silk jacket over her slim

14

hips. The corners of her fire engine red lips curled in a mocking smile. "Carlita. How are you?"

She extended a limp hand in Carlita's direction.

"I'm fine, Anjelica." Carlita inwardly winced as she took her sister-in-law's hand. "I must admit I'm a little surprised that you and Eddie made a special trip to Savannah for Tony's wedding."

Anjelica shot her husband a quick glance. "It's more a mixture of business and pleasure."

Eddie cleared his throat at his wife's comment. "It's all pleasure, Anjelica."

Carlita could tell from the tone of her brother's voice he was displeased at Anjelica's comment, and she felt a sudden uneasiness in the pit of her stomach. "You're not here for Tony's wedding. Did someone send you down here?"

"There is a little business matter. It ain't got nothin' to do with you. We're family. Can't I pay a visit to my family?"

"Oh, you're family all right."

Carlita forgot Mercedes was in the room until she stepped between Carlita and her brother. "It's nice to see you, Uncle Eddie. I'm sure you and Aunt Anjelica are exhausted after the long trip and want to go relax."

"Yeah. We gotta get going. We'll be here tomorrow around noon for the nuptials." Eddie placed a light hand on his wife's back and guided her toward the door. "Vito said Vinnie and Brittney will be arriving sometime today." He paused when he reached the door. "He staying here with you?"

"Who's asking? You or Vito?" Carlita asked.

"Maybe Vito. Maybe me," Eddie shrugged.

"Maybe not," Anjelica muttered.

Eddie jabbed a stubby finger at his wife. "You got a big mouth."

"You got a bigger mouth." Anjelica lifted her chin and turned to Carlita. "Congratulations on the upcoming wedding. It's nice to see you again, Carlita, even if I'm not a big fan of the south. Too many bugs and ridiculous heat. I'm goin' downstairs to smoke."

Anjelica stepped out of the apartment, her heels clattering on the stairs as she made her way down the steps.

Eddie muttered something unintelligible under his breath.

Carlita pinned her brother with a stare. "I don't want any crap goin' on at Tony's wedding, whether it's you, or Vito or even my son, Vinnie. This is Tony and Shelby's big day."

Eddie lifted both hands. "You got my word. I won't start anything as long as no one else gets it going."

"Eddie..." Carlita warned. "I will personally throw you out if you start trouble."

"You got my word."

Carlita followed her brother down the stairs and into the alley.

Anjelica stood on the stoop smoking. She blew a puff of smoke in her husband's face. "I'm hungry. You got any decent restaurants in this Podunk town?"

"The Parrot House Restaurant around the corner serves delicious food. My friend Pete Taylor owns it."

"What kind of food?" Anjelica took another drag on her cigarette before dropping it on the ground and grinding it with the tip of her shoe.

"The edible kind," Eddie smarted off.

"You're a jerk."

"I love you, too."

"They have a large menu. Burgers, wings, the typical pub fare. They also serve specialty dishes with a southern flair." Anxious to get away from her obnoxious sister-in-law and annoying brother,

Carlita backed into the hall. "I'll see you tomorrow. The wedding is at twelve o'clock sharp in the courtyard out front."

"We'll see you then." Eddie escorted his wife to the rental car before climbing behind the wheel and driving off.

Carlita started to close the door.

"Hey!" Elvira, Carlita's neighbor and former tenant, motioned to her from the doorway across the alley.

"What's up?"

"I wanted to ask you if there are any last minute instructions to go over for tomorrow." Elvira graciously offered her company's security services to oversee Tony and Shelby's wedding, claiming it was their wedding gift.

At first, Carlita dismissed the idea, but after giving it some thought, she decided it wouldn't be a bad idea to have someone keep an eye on the restaurant entrance. Elvira's presence would head off potential hungry customers from crashing the wedding reception.

"No. The wedding ceremony is at noon over in the courtyard. The reception will start right after the ceremony."

"Sounds good. Dernice offered to help out, too."

"It should be an easy job." Carlita remembered Eddie's words and Anjelica's mysterious comment, how her brother was in town to not only attend the wedding but also take care of a little business. "Or maybe not."

Elvira nodded in the direction of where Eddie's car had just pulled out. "Is that more of your mafia family showing up for the wedding?"

"What makes you think they're mafia?"

"The clothes. I know my designer duds. The chick was wearing a Marni dress. They cost a cool six hundred bucks minimum and the Jimmy Choo shoes." Elvira continued. "His suit wasn't cheap, either. He's not a looker like your sons, but he's kinda got some of your features."

Elvira studied Carlita's face. "Must be your sons have their father's looks. My guess is he's a relative of yours. You have the same close set eyes and pointed chin."

Carlita clenched her fists, resisting the urge to whack Elvira. She had enough going on without having to put up with the woman's nonsense. "Are you done insulting me and my family?"

"So he is related." Elvira clapped her hands. "I knew it! Man, I'm good."

"You're a pain in the butt. I have enough to do without standing here listening to you rattle on."

"Wait!"

Carlita slowly turned back. "Now what?"

"Someone left a box on your back step while you were gone." Elvira ran inside her apartment and returned, carrying a large brown box. "It looked like

21

it was going to rain. I thought it might be a wedding present or something and I didn't want it to get wet."

She handed the box to Carlita. "Whatever it is, it's not very heavy."

Carlita shook the box. It made a small rattling noise. "Thank you for picking it up. As annoying as you tend to be, I appreciate you offering your security services for Tony and Shelby's wedding. We'll see you tomorrow?"

"Absolutely." Elvira stepped back inside her apartment and closed the door.

Carlita wandered across the alley and up the steps. "Mercedes?"

Mercedes emerged from her room. "I'm sorry I didn't tell you about Uncle Eddie and Aunt Anjelica. Uncle Eddie wanted it to be a surprise."

"It was a surprise all right." Carlita perched on the edge of the sofa, still holding the box.

"What's that?"

"I don't know. Elvira found it on our back stoop. She thought it might be a wedding gift and didn't want it to get wet."

Mercedes joined her mother. "Well? Open it up."

"If it is a wedding gift, maybe we should give it to Tony and Shelby."

"Then they should've addressed it to Tony and Shelby."

"True." Carlita eased her fingernail under the corner of the packing tape. She ripped the tape off and flipped the flaps.

Inside was another smaller box. "Garlucci" was scrawled across the front in big, black letters. She picked it up and gave it a gentle shake.

"Is there a return address?" Mercedes reached for the larger empty box. "No. Nothing."

Carlita frowned. "Maybe it's not for the wedding." A troubled feeling settled over her, an inkling she wasn't going to like what she found inside.

"Here. You open it." She handed the box to her daughter. "I'm gettin' a bad feeling about this."

"Maybe it's a mini bomb." Mercedes pried the tape off and reached into the smaller box. "What in the world?"

Chapter 3

"It's a miniature bride and groom...a cake topper." Mercedes gingerly removed the figurine. On closer inspection, she noticed something was missing. "The groom's head is missing."

Sure enough, the intact bride clutched the hand of a headless groom.

"Maybe there's something written on the outside of the smaller box, and we missed it." Carlita carefully inspected the box. "It could be the package got damaged in shipping, and the groom's head broke off."

She removed the brown packing paper. The groom's missing head was not inside.

"Well, that blows my theory," Mercedes said. "Why would someone mail a bride and groom cake topper with the groom's head missing?"

"Maybe Eddie is playing a sick joke on Tony." Carlita reached for her cell phone and tapped out a message to her brother, asking if he had left a box on the back stoop. "I wonder if Elvira's surveillance camera picked anything up."

Carlita's cell phone beeped. Instead of Eddie, it was Vinnie, telling his mother Brittney and he had exited the highway and stopped for gas. His text ended with him telling his mother there was something important he needed to discuss with the family and wanted to make sure everyone was around.

"I don't like the sound of this." Carlita dialed her eldest son's number and waited for him to pick up. "You're not springing another surprise on me, are you?"

"No. No surprise this time. More of a complicated matter." Vinnie sounded distracted. "I'd rather not get into it over the phone in case someone is listening in. You know?"

A chill ran down Carlita's spine, and one word popped into her head...mafia. The family. "You're not bringing trouble to Tony's wedding, are you? Cuz we got our hands full without having to worry about family friends crashing the wedding."

"Like I said, I'll talk to you when I get there. Brittney and I will be there in ten minutes, fifteen tops." Before Carlita could reply, Vinnie disconnected the line.

She frowned at the phone.

"Now what?" Mercedes watched her mother set the cake topper on the coffee table. "What did you mean by family friends?"

"Vinnie said he wants to have a meeting when he gets here. He has something important to talk to us about."

"We can rule out Vinnie eloping, and his new wife being pregnant," Mercedes joked. "What else could there be?"

"I don't know." Carlita headed to the kitchen while Mercedes kept an eye on the alley.

"He's here," Mercedes said. "I'll run down to let them in, and see if Tony has a second to spare while I'm at it."

Carlita watched through the window as her daughter greeted her older brother before giving Brittney a quick hug. The trio disappeared from sight, arriving on her doorstep a couple of minutes later with Tony in tow.

She gave Brittney a warm hug and took a step back. "You're absolutely glowing, although not even showing."

Brittney patted her nearly flat stomach. "I've been waitin' every day for the baby bulge to appear, but nothing yet."

Vinnie wrapped his arms around his mother and hugged her tight. "You look great, Ma."

"Thanks. All of this running around trying to get the restaurant ready for the grand opening, not to mention helping out with the wedding have kept me on my toes." Carlita, not one to mince words, got down to business. "What's this important matter you need to discuss?"

Carlita's sharp eye didn't miss the uneasy glance Vinnie and his new bride exchanged. "What is it, Son?"

"We...gotta coupla unexpected extra guests attending the wedding and reception."

"What do you mean - unexpected guests?"

"Daddy insisted two of his personal bodyguards accompany us on this trip," Brittney said. "They're outside."

Carlita stepped over to the living room window and peered into the alley below. She caught a glimpse of a tall man, wearing a three-piece suit and standing on the stoop. "He wouldn't happen to be a burly man in a suit wearing a white fedora?"

"That's Luigi," Brittney nodded.

"I thought you said there was more than one."

"Ricco went around front. He's guarding the entrance to the pawnshop."

Mercedes peered over her mother's shoulder. "Why do you need bodyguards?"

Tony, who had remained silent so far, spoke. "I don't want any trouble at my wedding, Vinnie. Why are Vito's goons here?" He turned to Brittney. "No offense."

"None taken," Brittney replied. "It's for all of our safety and protection."

"Vito's got a hit on him, or maybe someone close to him. As an extra precaution, he sent two of his bodyguards down to keep an eye on us." Vinnie went on to tell his mother Vito suspected another "family member," Louie Esposito, had taken out a hit, with rumors it might take place while the couple was in unfamiliar surroundings.

Carlita slowly made her way across the room, her eyes drawn to the headless wedding topper. "Elvira found this on our back stoop a little while ago. We have no idea who sent it."

"It's a wedding cake topper," Vinnie shrugged. "So Tony's wedding cake topper got busted."

"That's not ours." Tony picked it up. "Could be Shelby ordered it before we found a topper with a man, woman and little girl on it. She can send it back since it's broken."

"The head is missing," Mercedes said bluntly.

"Missing?" Tony asked.

"Yeah. The head was off when we got it. It isn't inside the box."

"That's creepy." Brittney shivered.

"It may be some sort of warning," Carlita said quietly. "But if this is a warning, then Tony is the target."

"I dunno, Ma. We ain't had no trouble around here. The first thing to do is find out if Shelby ordered a cake topper. Let me check real quick."

With the topper in hand, Tony exited the apartment. He returned a short time later. "Shelby said she never ordered a topper. Where's the package it came in?"

Mercedes handed the boxes to her brother.

"I don't know what to think. Seems to me someone went to a lot of trouble to leave a broken cake topper on our doorstep."

"Maybe it's your Uncle Eddie playing a practical joke."

Vinnie's head shot up. "What's this about Uncle Eddie?"

"He's here. He showed up on our doorstep a couple of hours ago," Tony said. "He wanted to surprise us."

"What a scumbag."

Carlita pressed a hand to her chest, taken back by the hard tone in Vinnie's voice. "Your Uncle Eddie is a scumbag?"

"He's not supposed to be here. Vito told him to stay put. Wait'll Vito finds out Eddie is down here."

"Now I'm really confused." Carlita shook her head. "Your Uncle Eddie and Aunt Anjelica are here for Tony's wedding."

"I wouldn't bet my life on it."

Brittney grasped her husband's arm. "I'm sure Daddy already knows Eddie is here."

"Which means there could be even more members of the family hanging around now," Vinnie pointed out. "Half the family will be down here before we know it." He ran a ragged hand through his hair. "There's not much we can do about it now, except to keep our fingers crossed and hope for the best."

"Why can't I have a normal family?" Frustrated, Carlita marched to the kitchen to fix a pot of coffee and clear her head. The last thing she needed was the mafia on her doorstep...again!

At the very least, Vinnie should've given her a heads up about what was afoot. Carlita squeezed her eyes shut. Not only did she have to worry about making sure the wedding went off without a hitch, she now she had to worry about a hit on her son and daughter-in-law's lives.

"I'm sorry, Mrs. Garlucci."

Carlita's eyes flew open. "It's okay, but please don't call me Mrs. Garlucci. It's either Carlita or Ma."

"Carlita." Brittney smiled hesitantly. "I think Daddy is being over-protective. I'm sure the wedding will be fine. In fact, I would like to help. Just tell me what to do."

"Thank you, Brittney. That's very sweet. Are you thirsty? I have some bottled waters in the fridge, or sweet tea if you're interested." While pouring drinks, Carlita kept the conversation light. They talked about life in New Jersey, Brittney and Vinnie's recently renovated apartment and the baby.

34

They finished pouring the drinks. Carlita carried them into the living room while Brittney set a plate of cookies on the coffee table.

"How is Shelby this afternoon?" Carlita turned her attention to Tony.

"Better. She was getting ready to head out to run some errands with Violet."

"Is there something wrong with Shelby?" Vinnie grabbed a cookie off the plate.

"She's been feeling under the weather. I think she's stressed out between the wedding, working and trying to pack up and move to the new apartment." Tony glanced at his watch. "I can show you around the restaurant and the apartment before I head back to the pawnshop."

The siblings downed the rest of their snacks and drinks and headed into the hall. Carlita told them to go ahead without her, explaining that she wanted to try to reach Eddie on his cell phone to try to get to the bottom of the broken cake topper.

After several attempts, she was finally able to reach her brother, who insisted he never sent a cake topper.

Carlita ended the call and wandered into the hall. The apartment door catty-corner to their unit opened, and Sam Ivey, her newest tenant, emerged.

"Hello, Sam."

"Hello, Carlita. How are the last minute wedding plans going?"

"Ugh." She rolled her eyes. "I've got my hands full. My eldest son and his wife just arrived. I'll introduce them to you later. My brother, Eddie, and his wife arrived unannounced."

"And uninvited?" Sam guessed.

"You could say that. We're going to have a full house around here. I hope we won't be too disruptive."

"You aren't going to bother me."

"You're still coming to the wedding tomorrow?"

Sam hesitated.

"Sam..." Carlita's tenant originally rsvp'd he would be attending, having gotten to know Shelby, Violet and Tony since moving in.

As a wedding gift, Sam had taken them on a tour of historic downtown Savannah, something even Violet seemed to enjoy, especially after stopping off at Leopold's for ice cream.

The problem was Mercedes. Her daughter and Sam had been at odds from the moment they laid eyes on each other. Surprisingly, the majority of the animosity had been on Mercedes' part.

Carlita suspected her daughter was attracted to the handsome former cop, turned tour guide.

Both had called a truce, but there was still an undercurrent of tension between them. Mercedes was always quick to take off whenever Sam made an appearance.

"You are coming to the wedding?" Carlita pressed.

"Of course." Finally, Sam nodded. "There's no way I'm going to miss an authentic Italian wedding feast."

"Good." Carlita and Sam descended the stairs and stopped when they reached the bottom. "You wouldn't happen to have noticed someone out back, dropping off a package earlier today, would you?"

Sam shook his head. "No. I just got back from a group tour and there weren't any packages on the steps."

"I guess Elvira had already picked it up by then."

"I'll see you later." Sam gave Carlita a jaunty wave and sauntered off.

"Ma!" Mercedes bolted from the back of the restaurant and jogged towards her.

"You just missed Sam," Carlita teased. "Where are your brothers?"

"Inside the restaurant. You gotta come quick."

"Why?" Alarmed, Carlita followed her daughter down the alley. "Is something wrong?"

"Yeah. You gotta see this for yourself."

Chapter 4

Carlita's heart plummeted as she stepped into what *had* been her sparkling clean, shiny new commercial kitchen, her favorite area of the restaurant. "What happened?"

"It looks like someone broke in, lookin' for something." Vinnie pointed to the back door and splintered doorframe. "They weren't very good at it, either."

Sudden tears welled up in Carlita's eyes. It was all too much. She could handle the stress of the last minute running around. She could handle having her brother show up on her doorstep.

She could even handle Vito's goons hanging around to protect her family members. What she couldn't handle was knowing someone intentionally broke into her restaurant and tore the place apart.

Carlita slumped against the stainless steel counter. A pan teetered on the edge and fell to the floor. It was the last straw, and she burst into tears.

"It's okay, Ma. We'll get this place cleaned up in a jiff." Mercedes put her arm around her mother's shoulders.

"Yeah. It's not too bad." Brittney cleared the counters while Tony headed to the front of the restaurant to check for damages.

Vinnie and his sister began putting away the pots and pans. "We got this. Don't worry."

"You're right. It's not too bad." Carlita swiped at her tears. "I guess I'm just stressed out."

Tony rejoined them. "The front of the restaurant is fine. It looks like they tried to get into the cash register, gave up and left."

The siblings made quick work of cleaning up the mess while Carlita's middle son ran next door to grab his toolbox. Upon returning, Tony installed an extra deadbolt he found in the pawnshop and was even able to repair the damage to the back door.

"It's just some two-bit thieves," Vinnie assured his mother. "They probably got ticked off when they couldn't find any cash and made a mess."

"Right." Despite her son's words of encouragement, Carlita wasn't convinced.

"You gonna file a police report?" Tony asked.

Carlita hung the pot on the hook and glanced around. "Nothing appears to be missing. I'm not sure what I would report, other than having it on record the place was broken into. It's just one more thing to deal with."

Despite her children encouraging her to file the report, Carlita decided against it, hoping whoever broke in wouldn't try it again since they hadn't been successful.

After finishing up, Tony headed back to work.

Vinnie and Brittney decided to take the trolley to the City Market for some shopping and to grab a quick bite to eat.

The rest of the afternoon passed in a blur. Paulie, Gina and the kids showed up around dinnertime. Carlita ordered enough pizza for the entire family, and they all gathered in the restaurant's dining room.

"This place looks nice, Ma," Paulie said. "We're looking forward to tomorrow and seeing Ravello's Ristorante in action."

Gracie and Noel, bored with the adult conversation, began running around the tables until Noel tripped on a rug, skinned her knee and she started to cry.

"We better get the kids settled in at the hotel." Gina picked up her whining child. "I'm sure you're exhausted and tomorrow is gonna be a long day."

Carlita cast a concerned glance at a pale Shelby. "Shelby, you better get some rest, too."

"I am exhausted." She reached for Tony's hand as she glanced around the table at her soon-to-be family. "Thank you for coming all this way to celebrate with Tony and me. Thank you for all you've done to help make our day special."

Shelby wiggled out of her chair. She reached for the edge of the table when she began to sway.

"Whoa!" Tony reached out to steady her. "We're gonna get goin'. I'll stop by Ma's later to say good-night."

Tony was still holding onto Shelby as she and Violet stepped into the hall. Vinnie followed them to the door, locking it behind them. "Shelby looks kinda sickly."

"I agree." Carlita briefly told them of her concern, that there was something more going on with Shelby other than a simple case of exhaustion. "She has a doctor's appointment scheduled right after she and Tony return from their honeymoon."

Paulie, Gina and the kids were the next to leave. They headed out the back door to the alley and their rental car. Paulie helped his wife and children into the car before returning to his mother's side.

"I'm sorry you're not staying with us, Paulie."

"Not with this tribe," he grinned. "Besides, you got your hands full. Maybe next time, when you don't have a wedding to help coordinate and a reception to handle, we'll stay with you."

"I would like that." Carlita smiled at her youngest son. "You and Gina...everything okay?"

"We're doing good, Ma. Better than ever. My side business is taking off. I haven't resigned from my position as mayor." Paulie shrugged. "But if things keep steaming along, it's only a matter of time."

"I'm happy for you - for all of you," Carlita said softly. "Your father would be proud."

"I hope so."

Gina tapped the car horn and jabbed her finger toward the backseat, where Paulie Jr. had crawled into the back window.

"You better go. We'll see you in the morning." Carlita and Mercedes waited until Paulie and family were gone before slowly wandering back to the apartment. "Paulie's kids are a handful."

"Yes, but he and Gina seem happy." At least Carlita didn't have to worry about her youngest son. Now all she needed to do was get through tomorrow and focus on getting her restaurant up and running.

Carlita stopped by Tony's old apartment to check on Vinnie and Brittney.

Tony had already moved into the new three-bedroom apartment above the restaurant, to free up his old efficiency, so his older brother and new wife would have a place to stay.

After Vinnie assured his mother they were fine, she stopped to check the back entrance and caught a glimpse of Luigi, one of Vito's men, standing on the stoop smoking a cigarette.

He gave her a curt nod, and she sighed heavily.

"He still out there?" Mercedes stood at the top of the stairs, waiting for her mother.

"Yep. I'm sure the other one is close by too." Carlita trudged up the steps. "I'm not sure if it makes me feel safer or not."

"Me, either."

Exhausted, Carlita made a beeline for the bathroom while Rambo patiently waited at the foot of the bed.

Despite being tired, she tossed and turned all night. She dreamt of Vinnie - that he was there with her, but when she tried to talk to him, he disappeared.

Finally, early the next morning, after dreaming she'd opened the restaurant and no one showed up, she crawled out of bed and headed to the kitchen to start a pot of coffee.

Carlita waited for the coffee to finish brewing and then carried her cup onto the balcony. Rambo followed her out and flopped down next to her on the deck.

She sipped the hot brew, mentally ticking off the endless list of last minute details she needed to take care of. If Carlita could hold everything together until the celebration was over, everything else would be a piece of cake.

Despite having the support, encouragement and input of her children, Carlita was nervous about the restaurant's opening.

Tony's hands were full running the pawnshop. Mercedes was helping screen prospective tenants for Shelby's apartment, not to mention helping her brother run *Swag in Savannah*.

Mercedes was also hard at work editing her new book, *Omerta, Honor Among Family,* another thriller novel about life in a mob family.

Carlita tried to persuade her daughter to find something else to write about, certain that someday, someone up north would catch wind of her daughter's new hobby and come down to pay another visit.

As if she didn't have enough contact with the family...which brought her to the troubling presence of Vito's "bodyguards" she suspected were somewhere nearby.

She thought about the cake topper with the missing head. Was it a veiled threat? Tony was not involved in Vito's business, at least not anymore.

Carlita reminded herself Vito's goons would be on hand. Elvira and Dernice would secure the entrance to the restaurant/reception venue. Perhaps things would run smoothly and she was worrying about nothing.

The smell of cigarette smoke drifted up. Carlita peered through the railing spindles and caught a glimpse of a man standing on the stoop, smoking a cigarette. It was one of Vito's "employees."

As if sensing he was being watched, the man looked up.

Carlita quickly leaned back. "C'mon Rambo. Let's head inside. I'll throw some clothes on, and we'll go for a walk."

Rambo patiently waited while Carlita pulled on a pair of sweatpants and t-shirt. She grabbed her cell phone and apartment keys on the way out.

When they reached the alley, the man was still standing on the stoop. Their eyes met. "Hello, Vinnie's friend."

"Mrs. Garlucci," he drawled. "Gonna be a beautiful day for a wedding."

"I hope so..." Her voice trailed off.

"Luigi - Luigi Baruzzo."

"Luigi. Would you like some coffee?"

Carlita could've sworn he almost smiled. "No thank you, Mrs. Garlucci. Ricco is on his way to pick up some food now."

"I see." She motioned to her pooch. "I'm going to take Rambo for a walk."

Rambo let out a low growl, and Carlita whisked her pooch off the stoop. She could feel the heat from Luigi's eyes boring into her back until she rounded the corner and they were out of sight.

They kept a brisk pace, walking down the sidewalk and past the pawnshop. She paused in front of the courtyard where Tony and Shelby's ceremony would take place. Beyond that was the entrance to her restaurant.

From the upper level, she could see a flicker of light coming from Tony and Shelby's new apartment.

Rambo and she kept walking; stopping long enough for her to take a quick peek in the front windows of Ravello's, to make sure there wasn't another break-in.

They finished circling the block, walking past the front entrance of Elvira's apartment building and finally the alley where they began.

She was relieved to find Luigi gone.

Mercedes was sitting at the dining room table when Carlita stepped inside. "Hey, Ma."

"Hey, Mercedes." She looped Rambo's leash over the key rack and wandered into the kitchen to wash her hands. "You want something to eat?"

"Cereal is fine." Mercedes shifted in her chair. "I figured I would get up early to help you with any last minute details. The hairdresser is arriving around nine to start on Shelby's hair, then mine and Fran's hair."

"Is Violet having her hair done?" Carlita asked.

"Yes. She mentions it to me every time I see her. You sure you don't want to get your hair done, too?"

"This mop?" Carlita smoothed her hair. "I'll stick with doing my own."

After breakfast, the women got to work adding some final courtyard decorations. They moved into Ravello's dining room to add the finishing touches.

Carlita's new kitchen crew arrived a short time later to start prepping the food.

Dominic, her restaurant manager, arrived around the same time. They went over the final details; then Mercedes and she returned to the apartment.

Carlita was able to knock everything off her to-do list, but it left her with barely enough time for her to slip into her dress and join the rest of the family in the courtyard for the ceremony.

Paulie and Mercedes were the first to enter. Mercedes' stunning cobalt blue dress fit her like a glove and accentuated her jet-black locks. They joined Tony and the pastor, who stood near the front.

Vinnie and Shelby's maid of honor, Fran, were next.

When Violet appeared, Carlita's heart melted at the sight of her soon-to-be granddaughter.

She pranced onto the red carpet and reached into the basket she was holding. Violet counted out a handful of flower petals and tossed them onto the ground.

The guests chuckled as she took two steps and repeated the process...counting and tossing, counting and tossing.

When she ran out of flowers, she skipped the rest of the way to the front and reached for Mercedes' hand.

The wedding march began. Shelby and her Uncle Jerry appeared in the doorway.

Shelby's princess V-neck dress was breathtaking. All eyes were on the beautiful bride as she and her uncle made their way to the front of the courtyard.

Carlita's throat clogged. If only her Vinnie could be here with her. If only he could see for himself that she was keeping his last dying wish, to get his children out of the family.

Would Vinnie approve of Shelby and Violet? She believed he would have. He would have been proud of his son...his sons.

Her heart swelled with pride as she gazed at her children, standing at the front, waiting for Shelby to join them and become a member of the Garlucci family.

A lone tear trickled down Carlita's cheek, and she swiped it away. The Good Lord had blessed the Garlucci family, despite the heartbreaking loss of her husband. She was thankful for all of her blessings...her health, her children, her grandchildren, her friends.

Shelby and her uncle reached the front, and the pastor spoke. "Who gives this woman to be married to this man?"

"Her aunt and I do." Shelby's uncle gently kissed his niece's cheek. When he turned, Carlita noticed his cheeks were wet.

The vows were quick, followed by a few words the couple spoke to each other. They exchanged rings as the pastor pronounced them husband and wife. "You may kiss your beautiful bride."

The passionate kiss got a few hoots and hollers, followed by applause. "Ladies and gentlemen, it's my pleasure to introduce Tony and Shelby Garlucci."

The applause continued as Tony picked Violet up and the trio strolled down the center aisle to the back of the courtyard.

Carlita eased past the guests, who stopped to congratulate the newlyweds. While the couple greeted the well-wishers, she hurried to the kitchen to check on the food and beverages.

A harried Dominic met her at the door.

"The wedding ceremony just ended. The guests will be ready for appetizers and drinks to start making their rounds in the next ten minutes or so."

"Of course." Dominic nodded. "I hate to be the bearer of bad news, Mrs. Garlucci. We have a small problem."

Chapter 5

"What kind of problem?"

"The risotto croquettes, they are very bland. Here, try one." Dominic grabbed a set of tongs and picked up one of the fried balls.

Carlita bit the side. A burst of hot steam poured out, along with the fragrant aroma of her special Italian spices. The rich fontina cheese mingled with the salty goodness of the ham melted in her mouth.

"This is delicious Dominic." Carlita popped the rest of the morsel in her mouth. "It doesn't taste bland at all."

"Are you sure?"

"Absolutely. Don't forget the sun dried tomato sauce. It will give the dish a nice pop."

"You must sample the rest of the appetizers as well." Dominic lifted a tray off the table. "Please."

Carlita's keen eye honed in on the presentation. She had hand-picked the menu, from the chicken parmesan sticks, risotto croquettes and mini Italian cheese rolls for appetizers to the spaghetti and meatballs, lasagna stuffed shells and mini pizza pies for the main entrees.

Dessert consisted of bite-size cheesecakes, tiered trays of Nonna Garlucci's Italian cookies, and of course, the wedding cake Shelby and Tony selected.

She'd asked for the couple's input for the menu. Both insisted they wanted her to make the final decision.

Carlita finished taste testing the appetizers, giving them her seal of approval before returning to the courtyard to join her children.

Pirate Pete and Victoria "Tori" Montgomery stood outside the gate. She also spotted Glenda and Mark Fox. Autumn, a family friend, was also nearby. Autumn's brother, Steve, stood talking to Cool Bones.

The Walton Square neighbors were in attendance, as were the pawnshop employees, several of Tony's associates, Mercedes' group of author friends and many more familiar faces.

Carlita had also invited several of the local restaurant owners, a few she'd gotten to know since joining the Savannah Area Restaurant Association. Pirate Pete Taylor was also a member.

A beaming Tony and his beautiful bride, along with Violet, made their way into the restaurant. Carlita trailed behind, passing by a couple of servers who were making their rounds, offering drinks and goodies to the guests milling about.

Elvira, clad in a crisp, navy blue security uniform, stood near the restaurant entrance. She slipped something into her pocket as Carlita approached.

"What was that?"

"What was what?"

"In your pocket. I saw you slip something into your pocket."

"It was nothing."

Carlita held out her hand. "Let me see nothing."

"All right." Elvira reluctantly reached into her pocket. She pulled out a stack of business cards and dropped one of them into Carlita's hand.

"What's this?"

"What does it look like?"

"Business cards." Carlita flipped it over. "EC Security Services. No job too big or too small." She waved the card in Elvira's face. "You're handing out business cards to the wedding guests?"

"Sort of."

"How do you 'sort of' hand out cards?" Carlita asked. "Either you are, or you aren't."

"I am. You didn't tell me I couldn't. Besides, I'm doing this gig for free when I could be out making money somewhere else."

"Oh, brother." Carlita cast her eyes skyward. "Why am I surprised?" She leveled her gaze. "This is tacky."

"Tacky schmacky. I've already got a handful of interested parties."

A couple approached, someone Carlita didn't recognize. "Welcome. I'm Carlita Garlucci. You're friends of Shelby?"

"We're friends of both Shelby and Tony," the woman replied. "Unfortunately, we're running a little behind and missed the wedding ceremony."

"The couple is inside greeting guests," Carlita said.

Elvira held out a card. "EC Security Services is handling the wedding security. We're on call twenty-four hours a day. There's no job too big or too small for EC Security."

The man gave Elvira an odd look. He dropped the card in his pocket and followed the woman inside.

"Elvira," Carlita hissed. "That's enough."

"Fine. I'm running out of cards anyways. You got more people at this shindig than I thought you would. I didn't know you knew that many people."

"Well, I do. Now try to behave yourself. I'll ask one of the servers to swing by with some hors d' oeuvres." Carlita glanced behind her. "Where is Dernice?"

"She's covering the other side," Elvira said. "Don't forget the champagne."

"I'll have them bring some goodies to Dernice, too." Carlita eased past Elvira.

"Wait." Elvira stopped her. "Who are the two goons hanging around? I saw one of them camped out on your back step last night and again this morning. A few minutes ago, I saw the other one pacing up and down the block, like he was casing the joint."

"They're...friends of my son, Vinnie," Carlita said. "They won't bother you. Just don't try to give them a business card."

"Too late. The one with the weird white hat looked at me like I had two heads." Elvira lowered her voice. "They're mafia, aren't they? I can peg a mobster a mile away."

"Unbelievable," Carlita muttered under her breath. "I'll go track down a server."

"Don't forget the champagne," Elvira hollered.

"No drinking on the job." Carlita stepped back inside and nearly collided with one of the servers, stationed near the door. "Could you please take some goodies to the security guards?"

"Elvira Cobb?" The woman grinned.

"Don't tell me...she gave you a business card, too."

The woman chuckled and patted her pocket. "No worries. I'm headed outside since a number of guests are mingling out in the courtyard, enjoying this beautiful summer day."

She headed to the exit with her tray full of goodies.

Carlita scanned the crowd, searching for the bride and groom, and found them near the head table, talking to Pirate Pete.

The DJ, a man Steve Winter recommended, began to speak. Carlita half-listened as he announced the bride, groom and Violet, telling everyone dinner would begin shortly.

"Am I late?" Carlita spun around to find her new friend and trolley driver, Reese, standing behind her.

"Not at all. We're still in the midst of the pre-meal festivities." Carlita led Reese to one of the servers, who loaded a small plate with tempting treats.

"These look delish." Reese picked up a chicken parmesan stick and nibbled the end. "Oh, man. This is good stuff." She took a big bite. "Well? How was the ceremony? Did you bawl your eyes out? I know when my son got married I bawled like a baby."

"No, I did get teary-eyed. We love Shelby and are excited to have her as a part of our family, and of course Violet." Carlita nodded toward the entrance. "Did you see Elvira?"

"You can't miss her. She tried to give me a business card and then when she realized it was me, she snatched it right out of my hand." Reese laughed. "I told you about the time we had a run in, didn't I?"

"Yes, and I don't doubt it for a minute." Carlita placed a light hand under Reese's elbow. "Have you met my son, Tony? I don't think he's ever been on the Big Peach."

The women crossed the room, and Carlita waited until Tony was free before introducing them.

Tony shook Reese's hand. "It's nice to finally meet you, Reese. My mom sure does enjoy riding the Big Peach." He turned to a beaming Shelby. "This is my wife, Shelby."

"How do you do." Shelby smiled warmly as she shook Reese's hand.

"You two make a snazzy couple." Reese elbowed Carlita. "You got some good lookin' kids right here, Carlita. Why if I was forty years younger and fifty pounds lighter...and your son wasn't married." She winked at Tony. "I might have given Shelby a run for her money."

"I'm Violet." Violet wiggled between her mom and Tony.

"Hello, Violet." Reese set her plate of food on the table and knelt down. "I love your name. Your dress is pretty. You look like a princess."

"Except when she's being naughty," Shelby said.

"I'm not naughty." Violet crossed her arms. "Who are you?"

"Reese drives the Big Peach," Carlita explained.

Violet's eyes widened. "You drive a peach?"

"It's the nickname for my trolley. Maybe Nana will take you on a trolley ride one day."

"Will you, Nana?" Violet tugged on Carlita's hand.

"Of course. We'll ride the Big Peach soon, maybe even while mommy and Tony are on their honeymoon," Carlita promised.

"See you later." Reese held up her hand for Violet to give her a high five and then slowly stood. "You're lucky, Carlita. You've got a nice family."

"I'm blessed," Carlita nodded. "I see my son, Paulie, and his family over there."

"Carlita." Sam Ivey quietly came up behind her and tapped her shoulder.

"Hello, Sam. I'm glad you could make it." Carlita noted a troubled look on his face. "Is something wrong?"

"Yes. I think you should come out to the courtyard. It's about one of the wedding guests."

Chapter 6

"A female guest collapsed. She's not responding, and her pulse is weak. I took the liberty of calling 911 and requested an ambulance."

Carlita and Sam dashed out of the restaurant. Reese, curious to find out what had happened, followed behind.

Vito's bodyguard stood sentinel at the gate, watching as they passed through. Carlita cast him a quick glance, wondering if he was somehow involved.

A small crowd had already gathered around the woman; including a woman who was screaming hysterically. "Megan! Megan! Can you hear me?" Her eyes scanned the crowd as tears streamed down her face. "Can someone please help?"

"An ambulance is on the way." Sam knelt next to the woman. "Is this your friend?"

"Yes. Megan was talking to this good-looking Italian guy, the best man in Tony and Shelby's wedding. I think it was Tony's brother." The woman paused.

"Go on."

"Well, they were making small talk. All of the sudden a blonde chick in a clingy pink dress showed up. She got in our faces, griping about us talking to him. After she left, I went to use the bathroom. When I got back, Megan started complaining she wasn't feeling well. Next thing I know, she collapsed."

"Does your friend have any medical conditions, a possible cause for her collapse?" Sam asked.

"Not that I know of." The woman's face crumpled. "Something is terribly wrong with her, isn't it?"

Off in the distance, Carlita could hear the faint wail of sirens. "Help is on the way."

Mercedes quietly crept up behind her mother. "What happened?" she whispered.

Carlita shook her head and motioned Reese and her daughter off to the side.

"Something suspicious is going on. According to the woman's friend, Vinnie was talking to them. Brittney showed up and caused a minor scene. Shortly after, the woman complained to her friend that she was feeling ill and then collapsed. Sam isn't saying it, but I think this woman is in rough shape."

"What do we do?" Mercedes whispered.

"First of all, Elvira needs to keep the guests inside the restaurant and away from the courtyard."

"I'm on it." Reese darted out of the courtyard.

Carlita eyed Vito's guy. "We need a record of everyone here in the courtyard. Can you take a quick video with your cell phone?" She gave a slight nod toward the door. "Make sure you include Vito's employee."

"His name is Ricco." Mercedes slipped her hand into her blouse and pulled out her cell phone.

"Mercedes." Carlita wrinkled her nose.

"What? I didn't have anywhere else to put it." She shifted off to the side and took a step back while Carlita hustled to the entrance. "Ricco?"

The man nodded. "Yes, Mrs. Garlucci."

"Could you do me a huge favor?"

"It's done."

"What's done?"

"I've secured the scene. I'm stopping anyone who tries to get in."

"Thank you."

"You're welcome." She turned to go and then turned back. "You didn't happen to see anything, did you?" Their eyes met.

"You did see something?"

"Maybe," Ricco said. Before he could elaborate, an ambulance barreled around the corner and screeched to a halt. Two EMTs sprang from the vehicle and ran toward the gate.

"In here." Carlita quickly led them to the young woman and Sam Ivey, who was still kneeling next to the woman's chair.

Sam briefly explained what had transpired and then made room for them to begin examining the unconscious woman. The men threw out medical mumbo jumbo, which went right over Carlita's head.

One of them made their way back to the ambulance and returned with a stretcher. Together, they gently loaded the woman onto it.

The EMTs exited the gate, passing by two police officers who had just arrived. Sam and the woman's friend joined them on the sidewalk, talking in low voices.

After a brief exchange, one of the officers entered the courtyard.

Carlita greeted him near the gate. "I'm the owner of this property."

"Ivy...er...Sam Ivey, told us Megan Burelli, the woman on her way to the hospital, was a wedding guest."

"Yes, although I don't know her personally. In fact, I didn't even know her last name. I believe she may be a friend of my son's new wife, Shelby Townsend. As far as we know, Ms. Burelli suffered some sort of medical incident."

"I got the call on my radio, and my partner and I stopped by to see if we could assist since we were in the vicinity." The officer rocked back on his heels. "For some reason, your address stuck in my mind. I'm pretty sure we've been called to this location a few times."

"What are you trying to say?" Carlita's eyes flashed in anger.

"Easy Nate." Sam placed a light hand on the officer's shoulder. "As a tenant of Mrs. Garlucci's, I can personally vouch for her and her family. Notwithstanding evidence, I don't believe they had anything to do with Ms. Burelli's unfortunate collapse."

"I didn't mean to ruffle feathers. You know the beat. We gotta cover all the bases." The young officer, Nate, extended his hand to Sam. "We miss you down at the precinct. You staying busy?"

"You betcha. Staying busy and having the time of my life," Sam said.

"Unless you need anything else, I have a wedding to celebrate." Carlita pinned Officer Nate with a pointed stare.

"Yes, ma'am. Hopefully, you won't be hearing from us again."

"But someone will let me know the status of Megan Burelli's condition?" Carlita asked.

"Of course."

Mercedes and Reese stood waiting for Carlita on the other side of the gate. "Well?"

"So far, it appears Ms. Burelli experienced some sort of medical episode." Carlita pressed a hand to her chest. "At least I hope that's what it was and that she'll be all right."

"Me too," Mercedes tapped the bodice of her bridesmaid's dress. "I got it."

"Got what?" Reese asked.

"I videotaped everyone inside the courtyard, just in case."

"Good girl." Carlita caught a movement out of the corner of her eye. She'd completely forgot about Ricco. "Mr. Ricco, I have to get back to my son's wedding. Before I do, I was wondering if you happened to witness the young woman's collapse."

"I did." Ricco nodded. "Course, that's my job...to keep an eye on everyone and everything, and especially Brittney and Vinnie."

"Yes, and I appreciate your...dedication to your job."

"Thank you." Carlita could've sworn Ricco smiled.

"So you saw what happened," Mercedes prompted.

"Yes. The woman and her friend were sipping champagne and eating some of the appetizers the servers brought around. Might I add that the food was delicious."

"Thank you," Carlita said. "And then what happened?"

"All of the sudden, the woman clamped a hand over her mouth. She fell backward onto the chair and then keeled over."

"Clamped a hand over her mouth?" Reese clarified.

"Yep. Like maybe she was choking on food or something," Ricco nodded.

"Great," Carlita groaned. "Maybe her friend had it wrong about what happened, and we *are* responsible."

"People choke on food all of the time," Mercedes pointed out. "You can't be held responsible for someone choking on a piece of food."

"Is there anything else?" Carlita asked.

"Nope." Ricco shook his head. "Other than the friend was screaming Megan's name over and over, real hysterical-like. That's when Sam Ivey, the former cop, showed up and took over. He's the one who called for an ambulance."

"How do you know it was Sam?" Mercedes asked.

Ricco patted his pocket. "I know everyone who was invited to the wedding and cops, in particular, even former cops. It's part of my job to know who's around."

Carlita's jaw dropped. "You have information on every single person who was invited to my son's wedding?" It never occurred to Carlita that Vito would go as far as investigating the wedding guests. Then again, he and his "employees" were keeping an eye on his daughter.

"I do. Luigi and I both have a list. We went over it last night."

"I see."

Ricco lowered his gaze, causing Carlita to wonder if there wasn't something else. Something Ricco wasn't telling her. "You know Sam Ivey, my tenant, is a retired police officer and you know something else about the wedding guests."

Carlita continued. "Please, tell me what you saw or heard."

Chapter 7

"Ah, it's nothing." Ricco waved dismissively. "You pegged it right. The chick was chowing down, probably choked on an olive or something and keeled over."

Carlita suspected Ricco wasn't telling her everything. Despite her attempts to get him to talk, he refused to elaborate. She finally gave up, and the trio made their way back to Ravello's.

Mercedes remained silent until Ricco was out of earshot. "He was going to say something and suddenly changed his mind."

"Did you happen to notice his earpiece?" Reese whispered.

"He...uh, was probably staying in contact with his partner, Luigi." Carlita didn't dare elaborate, anxious to avoid answering too many questions about Luigi and Ricco.

"I figured maybe he was talking to Elvira and was part of her security team," Reese said.

"They're actually two different security companies."

Mercedes snorted, and Carlita shot her daughter a warning look.

"We...we weren't sure if Elvira and her sister had enough manpower to cover the event," Carlita fibbed.

"That's cool. I figured since Elvira wore an earpiece, too, they were working together."

"Elvira is wearing an earpiece?"

"Yep." Reese nodded. "It's one of those new-fangled contraptions. I've seen them on my crime scene investigation shows. Of course, you have to be on the same frequency to communicate."

The women began walking again.

"I hadn't noticed," Carlita said. "You've got a sharp eye, Reese."

"Thanks," Reese beamed. "A sharp eye and a vivid imagination." She started to say something else and then stopped.

"What were you going to say?"

"It's nothing." Reese's face turned bright red. "Just my brain working overtime."

"Does it involve Elvira?" Mercedes asked.

"No. It's about the other security guy. I'm sure it's nothing, you vetted him, and he's on the up and up."

Carlita said the first thing that popped into her head. "My son hired him." Which was close to the truth, in a roundabout way. "Did he say or do something?"

"No. He just looks kind of..."

"Kind of?" Carlita prompted.

"Mafia-ish. He has a gangster look. Like I said, I watch too many of the crime shows. I'm sure your son trusts him."

"Don't be so sure about that," Mercedes muttered under her breath.

"We're here." Carlita stopped near the restaurant entrance. She waited until Reese and her daughter were inside, and she and Elvira were alone. "How's it going?"

"Good. Heard there was an incident over in the courtyard. One of the wedding guests choked on a piece of food and keeled over."

"We're getting conflicting stories. I'm not sure if she choked or if it was something else. She complained to her friend of not feeling well before slumping over in a chair. She's on her way to the hospital." Carlita caught a glimpse of the earpiece Reese mentioned. "What's that?"

"What's what?"

Carlita rolled her eyes. "We've had this conversation once already. You're wearing an earpiece."

"Oh, that." Elvira let out a fake laugh. "I wear the earpiece to all of my jobs. I use it to communicate with the rest of my staff."

"Like Dernice?"

"Yep."

"Where is Dernice?" Carlita glanced around.

"She's around the corner."

"I see." There was a long moment of silence. "Is the earpiece capable of hearing someone else in the vicinity, someone who is also wearing an earpiece?"

"Maybe." Elvira shifted her feet. "Yeah. It's possible."

"Let's say, for example, my son's friends, who are also here to keep an eye on guests and are also wearing earpieces. Would you be able to hear them?"

85

"Could be," Elvira admitted.

Carlita knew her ex-tenant well enough to know she'd seen or heard something. She got right to the point. "What did you hear?"

Elvira's jaw tightened, and she stubbornly shook her head, a sure sign Carlita was onto something. "Elvira, you overheard something. What did you hear?"

"All right. So...I overheard the goons in the suits talking about the guests. Did you know they have a detailed list of all of the guests who are here? Who does that?"

The mafia. "A very thorough security detail?" Carlita offered. "They take their jobs seriously." *Or face Vito*, she silently added. "I'm looking for specifics...did Ricco or Luigi mention a specific person or event while you were eavesdropping?"

"I might've heard something. I'm not sure yet. We should discuss it later when no one else is in the vicinity." Elvira crossed her arms. "I was thinking...I came up with a great idea."

"What kind of 'great idea?'"

"I was wondering if it would be possible for me to place a small business card stand; maybe next to the hostess station to help me drum up some business." Elvira hurried on. "I got some special cards made up that I think would be perfect to hand out to your diners."

"You want to continue promoting your security services business in my restaurant and to my customers?"

"Yep...and EC Investigative Services," Elvira added. "I have some new double sided cards...EC Investigative Services on one side and EC Security Services on the other side. I would make it worth your while."

"Really?" Carlita lifted a brow.

"I could pay you a finder's fee. How does half a percent sound?"

"How generous."

"Don't knock it. Every penny adds up."

"I'll think about it," Carlita said.

"We can talk later about what I may have overheard." Elvira lowered her voice. "You never know who might be listening in. In the meantime, I'll keep my ears open."

Back inside, Carlita didn't have time to dwell on the new information. The wedding party and guests had already started eating. She filled her plate with food before making her way to her family's table.

She'd forgotten all about her brother and his wife, who were seated across the table.

Eddie waited for Carlita to sit. "Heard there was a little problem in the courtyard."

"Yes, one of the guests fell ill and was taken away in an ambulance." Carlita unwrapped her silverware and smoothed the napkin in her lap. "I hope she'll be all right."

"The food is delicious, Carlita." Anjelica took a bite of her lasagna. "I need to get your lasagna recipe."

"Thank you. I'm glad you're enjoying it." Carlita tasted a bite of each of the dishes and agreed her kitchen crew had done an excellent job of preparing the food.

While the guests ate, Tony and Shelby stopped by each of the tables, thanking the guests for joining them.

After finishing the food, the couple, along with Violet, made their way to the makeshift dancefloor for the family's first dance. Soon, other guests joined them while the busboys cleared the tables.

Carlita quickly finished her food. It was time to check on the young woman's condition, and have a brief chat with the kitchen staff.

She stopped by Pirate Pete's table where he, along with the other members of the Savannah area restaurant group, was seated.

She greeted Gil Cross, the owner of Monster Pizza, and Mike Russo, the co-owner of Russo's Italian Eatery, both of which were also located in Walton Square.

Pete eyed Carlita's shimmery purple wedding dress, and let out a low wolf whistle. "You look stunning."

Carlita could feel her cheeks warm, and she absentmindedly ran her hand along the silky material. "Thank you. Mercedes helped me pick it out." Embarrassed by the attention, she quickly changed the subject. "How was the food?"

"It was every bit as good as mine," Mike smacked his lips. "Your chicken parmesan sticks were my favorite, with the spaghetti and meatballs a close second."

"I second the chicken parmesan sticks," Pirate Pete said. "Everything was top notch." His expression grew serious. "We heard one of the guests was taken away by ambulance."

"Yes." Carlita nodded. "It appears she may have choked on a piece of food. I'm on my way to find a quiet spot to see if I can get an update on her condition."

"That's terrible," Gil Cross said. "Hopefully, it was an accident and not the food."

"Why would it be the food?" Carlita asked. "I don't see anyone else getting sick...unless you know something I don't."

"No," Gil said. "I'm sure the food was fine."

Carlita thanked them for the feedback and then made her way into the kitchen where she'd locked her purse in the desk drawer.

She stepped out back and called the number on the card the officer left, but no one answered, so she left a brief message.

"Mrs. Garlucci." Dominic, her new manager, stuck his head out the door. "Well? How was the food?"

"It was delicious. I'm getting rave reviews, even from other area restaurant owners." Carlita smiled. "You've done a great job."

Her cell phone beeped, and she recognized the officer's number.

"If you'll excuse me." Carlita stepped to the corner of the building and pressed the answer button. "Carlita Garlucci speaking."

"Hello, Mrs. Garlucci. This is Officer Nate Clousen with the Savannah Police Department returning your call."

"Yes, thank you for calling me back Officer Clousen. I was hoping you might have an update on the condition of Megan Burelli, the guest at my son's wedding."

"I do have new information. Unfortunately, it's not good."

Chapter 8

"She's in the ICU," Clousen said.

Carlita reached out to steady herself. "That's terrible. Do the doctors have any idea what happened?"

"It's still too soon to say," the officer admitted. "I'm sorry to have to give you this news at what should be a joyous occasion."

"There's no need to apologize. Thank you for the call, and please...keep me posted." After hanging up, Carlita stared blankly at the phone, her mind whirling.

Dominic, who was still standing in the doorway, spoke. "You got some bad news?"

"One of the guests experienced a medical episode. They took her to the hospital. That was the officer who was on the scene."

"I hope she's all right," Dominic said.

"We're still waiting on more information." Anxious to avoid giving too many details, Carlita quickly excused herself and returned to the reception.

She went through the motions of the celebration, all the while Officer Nate's words ringing in her ears that a young woman, her guest, was gravely ill. Should she tell Tony and Shelby what happened?

After several attempts to catch Shelby and Tony alone, she decided to wait until the reception ended.

The last official event was cutting the cake, and finally, the guests began to leave.

Among the last to leave were Pirate Pete and the group of Savannah restaurant business owners.

"Thank you for joining us." Carlita attempted a half-hearted smile.

"You're welcome. Thank you for inviting us." Pete leaned in for a hug. "Is everything all right?" he whispered in Carlita's ear.

"Not really. We can talk later." Carlita pulled away. "How are the Flying Gunner and your Pirates in Peril show faring?"

"Business is brisk. In fact, it's better than expected. Of course, summertime is one of the busier seasons in Savannah. We're booked at seventy-five percent for our weekday shows and almost a hundred percent on weekends."

"I thought that was the case and noticed long lines at the dock." Carlita and Rambo were regulars at Morell Park, a stone's throw from Gunner's Landing, where The Flying Gunner was docked and where guests boarded the boat for the "Pirates in Peril" show.

With the wedding and gearing up for the restaurant opening, Carlita hadn't found the extra time to take in the show, which included a cruise along the Savannah River. "I'm hoping now that the wedding is behind us, I can sneak over one afternoon. Should I make a reservation?"

"No reservation needed. We'll fit you in, matie," Pete winked. "Why don't you bring the whole family?"

"We could. Paulie, Gina and their children are in town for a few days. Mercedes and I will be watching Violet while Tony and Shelby take a short honeymoon. I bet my grandkids would love the show."

"Then what're you waiting for? Bring 'em all."

"I think I will." Carlita thanked him and the other local restaurant owners again for attending.

"You'll do a bang up business here. You're in a prime real estate spot, what with the new trolley stop right out front." Mike Russo patted Carlita's arm. "I'm sure there are plenty of patrons and enough room for both our Italian restaurants."

"And enough pizza eaters," Cross, the owner of Monster Pizza, chimed in.

"Thank you for all of your support," Carlita said gratefully.

"We'll see you at Wednesday's regular restaurant meeting?" Mike asked.

"Of course." Carlita waited for the trio to exit the building before turning her attention to the almost empty dining room. The busboys were hard at work clearing the remaining dishes left behind by the wedding guests.

Reese and Mercedes stood talking near the back, while Violet skipped circles around them.

Carlita joined them and grabbed Violet's hand. "Did you have a piece of cake?"

"Yes. I'm still hungry," she said. "Can I have another piece of cake?"

"I have a better idea. We'll grab some leftovers to take home including some leftover cake." Carlita picked up the small child and held her close. "Did you have fun at Mommy and Tony's wedding?"

Violet nodded. "I wish they could get married every day."

"Not me," Carlita groaned.

Vinnie, Brittney, Paulie, Gina and the kids wandered over.

Violet wiggled out of Carlita's arms, and the children scampered off to play.

"You heard anything else about the woman out in the courtyard?" Vinnie asked. "Ricco said they took her away in an ambulance."

"She's in intensive care. There's no news about the cause of her collapse yet."

"Oh no." Brittney's eyes grew wide. "I heard she was the same one who was flirting with Vinnie. I told her to knock it off, or I was going to have to ask her to leave."

"Are you sure you didn't knock her off, instead of telling her to knock it off?" Mercedes joked.

"Mercedes," Carlita chided. "I'm sure Brittney wouldn't hurt a fly." *Her father, Vito? He was another story.*

"Officer Clousen promised to call me as soon as he had more information."

The newlyweds wandered back inside and joined them. "The wedding and reception were wonderful," Shelby gushed. "I don't know how I can ever thank you enough for helping to make this one of the best days of my life."

"You're welcome." Carlita hugged her and then her son.

"We heard about Megan Burelli. Any word on her condition?" Tony asked.

"It's not good. She's in intensive care."

Shelby's eyes clouded. "I didn't know Megan well. She'd only just started working at the post office. She's a friend of Sierra's, another co-worker."

Reese consulted her watch. "I've got an evening shift to cover. I better hop to it and head to the trolley depot." She hugged Tony and Shelby, and then Carlita walked her to the door.

"Thanks for inviting me, Carlita. This is the most exciting thing to happen to me since I kicked Elvira off my trolley," she joked.

"You're welcome. I'll see you tomorrow morning, bright and early? I've got some stuff to return over on the other side of town."

"The Big Peach and I will be here at seven fifteen sharp." Reese gave Carlita a mock salute and strolled out of the building.

Carlita peered around the doorway, looking for Elvira. She didn't see her, so she wandered to the corner, but Elvira was gone.

She returned to the nearly empty dining room and could hear the clatter of pots and pans coming from the kitchen.

Carlita eased the swinging door open. Dominic's kitchen crew was gone. He and one other worker were the only ones left. "Before you put the food away, I would like to see if my kids want to take any leftovers."

"Of course." Dominic removed a pan of lasagna from the fridge and set it on the counter. "We have some lasagna, spaghetti and meatballs, a couple of pizzas and some cake left."

"Let me go round up the troops." Carlita returned to the dining room. "Time to load up on leftovers."

Violet ran over. "Cake! Cake!"

"We want cake too," Noel piped up.

"Cake it is," Gina smiled. "The cake was delicious. The food was delicious."

"I agree," Vinnie said. "My favorites were the appetizers."

Brittney patted her tiny tummy bulge. "I enjoyed everything except for the chicken parmesan sticks. I'm pretty sure there were crushed nuts in them, and I'm allergic to nuts."

"There aren't any chicken parmesan sticks left," Dominic said.

"The mini Italian cheese rolls were delicious," Brittney hinted.

"I'm sorry. All of the appetizers are gone," Dominic replied. "We have plenty of spaghetti and meatballs left."

"Waste not, want not." Carlita grabbed a stack of to-go containers and passed them out. Everyone loaded the containers with food, including Dominic and the employee.

While they loaded up, Carlita thanked them again and reminded Dominic he had a couple of days off before meeting again to go over the final details for the restaurant's Friday opening.

After Dominic and the employee left, Carlita checked to make sure the doors were locked. She caught up with her children in the alley. "What a long, but wonderful day."

"Yes, it was." Tony gazed down at his bride as he squeezed her hand.

"My feet hurt," PJ whined.

"These heels are killin' me, too." Gina ruffled her son's hair. "We better head back to the hotel."

"I want to go swimming." PJ clung to his mother's leg.

"I thought your feet hurt."

"They do."

"If you don't knock it off, you're going to get a nap instead," his mother threatened.

PJ began crying.

"That's it, Dad. Time to go." Gina hugged Tony, Shelby, Carlita and finally Mercedes. "Everything was wonderful. We'll call you tomorrow morning. Pirate Pete mentioned something about his Pirates in Peril show, and we thought we would take the kids."

"I want to go, too," Violet tugged on Carlita's hand.

"Then that's what we'll do. The weekend matinee show starts at one o'clock."

"Why don't we meet you there, Ma?" Paulie suggested.

"What about you, Vinnie and Brittney?" Carlita asked.

"We would love to, but we're going shopping at the outlet mall. I need to find some sensible shoes. Vinnie keeps telling me my stilettos are too high."

"Brit agreed to buy a pair of two-inch heels," Vinnie teased.

"But only until the baby comes." Brittney wagged her finger at her husband. "Then I'm gonna start wearing my heels again."

"Of course." Vinnie kissed his wife's cheek. "So we'll be shopping tomorrow. How 'bout we meet for dinner later instead?"

"Sounds good."

"We're gonna head out to grab some snacks. Brittney and the baby are craving potato chips and ice cream." Vinnie and Brittney made their way to their car.

Out of nowhere, a black sedan with tinted windows cruised into the alley. It was Vito's men. Ricco and Luigi followed Vinnie's car onto the street.

"I see Vinnie's bodyguards are still on it," Tony said. "Shelby and I are gonna go change, grab our bags and head out."

"At least the reception ended early, and you'll have plenty of time to get to your hotel."

The couple planned a short, two-day honeymoon, driving to Hilton Head, where they'd reserved a honeymoon suite at a beachside luxury resort.

The couple promised Violet they would take a longer, family honeymoon trip to Florida and Disney World later that fall.

Violet was excited about the trip but just as excited to be spending a couple of days with Nana Banana and Aunt Mercedes.

Tony and Shelby returned with their bags. Shelby dropped to her knees and pulled her daughter close. "We'll be back before you know it."

"I know." Violet nodded solemnly. "Nana and I will bake cookies for you while you're gone."

"We will?" Carlita laughed.

"Yes. I want to bake Nonna Garlucci Italy cookies."

"Italian Cookies," Carlita corrected.

"Yep. They're Mommy's favorite."

106

Shelby smiled. "And they're your favorite, too."

Violet wrapped her arms around her mother and then hugged Tony. "Bye-bye, Tony Baloney."

"See you soon purple cookie eater," he teased.

"I'm not purple."

"You're right. You're Violet." Tony gave his new stepdaughter a gentle hug and kissed the top of her head. "Behave for Nana."

Violet promised she would. Her lower lip trembled as her mother and Tony made their way to the car.

Anxious to distract the young child, Carlita handed the leftovers to her daughter and scooped Violet up. "Would you like to take Rambo for a walk? He's been stuck inside the apartment all day. I'm sure he misses us."

"I miss him, too."

"Why don't you and Aunt Mercedes go get Rambo, while I stop by Elvira's place?"

"Haven't you had enough of Elvira today?" Mercedes joked.

"More than enough. Unfortunately, Elvira may have valuable information on Megan's collapse. I want to know what she overheard."

Chapter 9

Carlita rapped sharply on Elvira's back door while Mercedes and Violet ran upstairs to get Rambo.

She caught a glimpse of movement through the window. Elvira didn't answer, so she knocked again, harder this time.

The door flew open. Elvira stood in the doorway, clad in a pair of paint-spattered sweatpants and a tie-dyed Grateful Dead t-shirt. A red bandana tied around her head completed the ensemble.

"You look comfy." Carlita said the first thing that popped into her head.

"I'm painting. It's my only free afternoon for the next week." Elvira leaned her hip against the door. "Are you here to critique my attire or did you need something?"

"I want to know what you overheard on your earpiece during the reception."

"Ah. I almost forgot." Elvira's expression grew thoughtful. "Now you've got an almost-dead wedding guest on your hands."

"How do you know..."

Elvira cut Carlita off. "I have my sources. Word on the street is she consumed tainted food."

"The story is spreading like wildfire?" Carlita pressed a hand to her forehead. "How did you find out?"

"In my line of work, you gotta have connections."

"Good grief." Carlita slumped against the wall. "She ate something at the wedding, something tainted."

"That would be my guess."

"As far as I know, no one else got sick. What if the health department shuts me down before I even open my doors?" Carlita felt nauseous at the thought that not only was it possible her food was the cause of a young woman's perilous condition, but that her dream of opening Ravello's might not happen.

She could feel herself growing hysterical. "What am I going to do?"

"I would wait until the cops show up, find out what they plan to do," Elvira suggested. "It's not like you intentionally poisoned the woman."

"Of course I didn't, but the authorities might not see it that way."

"This was a private event. Unless the family wants to pursue a lawsuit, they're going to have to prove you or your food was responsible."

Carlita started to pace. "Without samples of the food, they would have a hard time proving it." She remembered how she and her children had split the leftovers to take home.

She replayed the events in her mind, from the moment she first arrived in the courtyard after finding out about the young woman's condition. "Wait a minute. Megan collapsed during the cocktail hour."

"So maybe one of your delectable appetizers was responsible," Elvira said. "I have my doubts on the food as a whole being contaminated. I ate several tasty morsels of each, and I'm perfectly fine."

"That's debatable," Carlita muttered.

"What's that supposed to mean?"

Carlita ignored the question. "The only problem is we didn't have any appetizers left."

Elvira gave Carlita a funny look.

"You have leftover appetizers," Carlita guessed.

"Did I say that?"

"You didn't have to. Listen, I need the leftover appetizers." Carlita shoved Elvira aside and barged into her apartment. "Where are they?"

"I don't know what you're talking about."

"The appetizers." Carlita marched to the refrigerator and yanked the door open. There, sitting on the top shelf was a stack of Carlita's to-go containers. "You do have leftovers."

"You can't just barge in here and help yourself to my food. I planned to eat the leftovers for dinner."

"I'll swap you some of the leftover spaghetti and meatballs." Carlita pulled the containers from the fridge. Keeping a tight grip on the food, she marched to the door.

Elvira lunged forward in an attempt to grab the containers, but Carlita was too quick. She easily slipped away. "This is life or death."

"You don't need all of the food, just a sampling of each."

"Then I'll take a sample and bring the rest back." Carlita ran across the alley as Elvira called out for her to stop. She ignored the woman's pleas, ran upstairs and into the apartment.

"Ma?" Mercedes and Violet emerged from the hall. "We were on our way down. Violet needed to use the bathroom."

"That's fine. I have to take care of something. I'll be done in a couple minutes." Carlita split each of the leftover appetizers in half. She placed her half in storage containers and left Elvira's half in the to-go containers.

She added a generous helping of spaghetti and meatballs to one of Elvira's containers before returning to the alley.

Elvira's back door was ajar. Carlita tapped lightly. "Elvira? I have the leftover leftovers."

Elvira tromped out to meet her, an annoyed expression on her face.

"I only took half." Carlita held out the containers.

"Half my food. Did you replace it with the spaghetti and meatballs?"

"I did."

"I guess that'll have to do. The spaghetti and meatballs weren't my favorite. They were kinda bland."

"Then don't eat them," Carlita said. "Before I leave, I want to know what you overheard on your ear piece."

"Overheard?"

"You overheard Vinnie's friends, Ricco and Luigi. Ricco was the one standing near the courtyard gate. Luigi was out back, probably somewhere in the vicinity of where Dernice was working."

"Oh…that." Elvira waved dismissively. "It was probably nothing."

Carlita switched tactics. "I thought you wanted to cut a deal. You tell me what you overheard, and in exchange, I'll let you put some of your business cards at the restaurant's hostess station."

"I've given it some thought. It doesn't seem like a fair exchange."

"I agree. I'm being way too generous." Carlita decided to beat Elvira at her own game. "I'll let you put your business card stand by the station for one month."

"What?" Elvira's mouth dropped open. "That's not fair. I was thinking of a more permanent arrangement and throwing in a finder's fee."

"Take it or leave it."

"Fine." Elvira sucked in a breath. "They mentioned Megan Burelli, how she was flirting with your son, Vinnie, when he was alone, not that I can blame her. Your son is a real hottie, but his wife? She's got a temper."

"Your commentary isn't necessary. Let's get back to what you overheard."

"At first, there was a discussion about some blonde in the courtyard, talking to Vinnie. One of them insisted it was Brittney Garlucci and then all of a sudden, the one named Ricco was like, 'No. That's not Brittney. It's some other chick, flirting with Vinnie. They discussed getting rid of her. I thought they were talking about escorting her out of the courtyard. Next thing I know, an ambulance pulls up, and the woman they were discussing gets carried out on a stretcher."

"They said 'get rid of her'"? A chill ran down Carlita's spine. Had Ricco done something to the wedding guest to cause her to keel over?

"Yep." Elvira nodded. "Those were his exact words. He said 'Are you thinkin' we should get rid of her?'"

The color drained from Carlita's face. What if one of Vito's "employees" somehow managed to slip something into Megan's champagne glass...something potentially lethal?

The mob's preferred method of murder was gunning people down; although she knew they also resorted to other means of eliminating a "problem." Surely, they wouldn't have taken out an innocent woman because she flirted with the boss' son-in-law.

Besides, Brittney intervened and had taken care of the matter...or had she? Carlita wondered what Vito would do in a situation where his daughter's happiness was at stake.

"...so I kinda wonder if maybe that wasn't the case," Elvira said.

"I'm sorry. I missed the last part of what you said."

"No, I was just saying I didn't hear anything else after the discussion about getting rid of her. If they'd actually, you know, done the deed."

"Nana." Violet ran down the alley and flung herself at Carlita. "We took Rambo around the block."

Mercedes joined them. "We're done walking Rambo."

"That was quick."

"Violet told me that her legs are tired," Mercedes said. "Hello, Elvira."

"Hello, Mercedes, Violet," Elvira said. "You both looked classy for the wedding. You clean up nice." She pointed to the dress Violet was still wearing.

"I love my dress." Violet twirled in a circle. "I'm going to wear it until tomorrow."

"No, we're going to take it off later," Carlita said. "We should head home. My legs hurt too." She thanked Elvira for the information before telling her she could drop her business cards off on Sunday.

Carlita waited until they were in the apartment and Violet was watching television on the sofa to fill her daughter in.

"That's terrible." Mercedes shook her head. "You don't think Vinnie and Brittney's bodyguards did something to Megan, do you?"

"I hope not. I'm not sure how far Vito would go to make sure his daughter, the apple of his eye, is happy."

Mercedes drummed her fingers on the dining room table. "If she did eat something lethal, how would we know it was ours? No one else got sick."

"Unless it was a targeted contamination. I stuck some samples of Elvira's appetizers in the fridge, way in the back. Don't eat them." A sudden thought popped into Carlita's head. "Remember the headless cake topper? How there wasn't a return address? You don't think the two are linked, do you?"

"No, I mean it did seem odd to have someone drop off an anonymous, headless cake topper."

Carlita sprang from the chair. "The more I think about it, the more I wonder. First, we have the headless cake topper, and then the other day, someone broke into the restaurant, but nothing came up missing, and now a possible poisoning. What if these aren't random coincidences?"

"Uncle Eddie." Carlita marched to the kitchen and snatched her cell phone off the counter. "Not only did he show up uninvited, but he also showed up around the same time all of these things started happening. I'm going to get to the bottom of this."

She dialed her brother's cell phone number. He didn't answer, so she left a message, asking him to return the call. "He mentioned taking care of a small business matter. What if there was a hit on Vinnie and/or Brittney and his own uncle was the one in charge of taking them out?"

"Do you really think he would try to kill a family member?"

Carlita lifted a brow. "It depends on what 'family' you're talking about." She quickly dialed her son's cell phone.

"Hey, Ma."

"Are you downstairs in Tony's old apartment?"

"Nah. We're still shopping for munchies. Brit also found a designer baby boutique she wants to check out. What's up?"

"I think the young woman, Megan Burelli, became ill after eating food at the reception," Carlita blurted out.

"But no one else got sick."

"I don't have all of the pieces figured out. I'm beginning to wonder if someone wasn't targeting a specific person or persons...Brittney or you."

There was a long pause. "That's a stretch, Ma. I mean, it would have to be an inside job. You know all of your employees."

"I just met them." Carlita could feel herself becoming hysterical. "What if it was a setup?"

Vinnie and Brittney may have been the targets. The more she thought about it, the more it made sense. From what Carlita remembered, Megan was petite with light-colored hair, a woman who bore a striking resemblance to Brittney. What if someone was working on the inside, hired to take Brittney out, but they accidentally took out the wrong woman?

122

"Vito didn't send his guys to Savannah for the fun of it. He must have believed there was a credible threat. Something isn't sitting right," Carlita said. "Promise me you'll be careful." She stopped short of mentioning her brother's name.

"I'll put a call into Vito, to see if he thinks Louie Esposito sent someone down here. If it makes you feel better, I promise Brit and I will be extra cautious. Look, I gotta go. We ran into Uncle Eddie and Aunt Anjelica a few minutes ago. We're heading into a pub for a cold brew and snack. We'll see you a little later."

"Don't let them buy you a drink," Carlita yelled into the phone. It was too late. Vinnie had already disconnected the call.

Chapter 10

Carlita flung the phone on the table. "Your Uncle Eddie and Aunt Anjelica are with Vinnie and Brittney."

"I chatted with them for a few minutes at the wedding." Mercedes covered her mouth to stifle her yawn. "Uncle Eddie mentioned something about taking care of a small business matter."

"That's what I mean."

"What are you talking about?"

"What if Vinnie and Brittney are the business matter?" Carlita glanced at Violet, sprawled out on the sofa and engrossed in a cartoon. "I haven't heard a peep out of my brother since we moved to Savannah. Next thing I know, he's on my doorstep."

"He's family."

"My point exactly."

Carlita glanced at her watch. "I left some decorations in the hall I need to bring inside." She stepped into the hall, quickly sorted through the box of decorations and then slid the box inside the apartment.

"Your cell phone was beeping, Nana," Violet said.

"It was?" Carlita snatched it off the counter. She had missed two calls and a text, all from Reese. Her eyes squinted as she read the message. *Got an interesting story from one of the other trolley drivers. Call me.*

Carlita promptly dialed Reese's cell phone. It went right to voice mail. "Hey, Reese. I got your message. Call me back."

She carried the phone into the living room. Violet crawled onto her lap and placed her head on Carlita's shoulder.

Carlita smiled as she pulled her close. Tomorrow, they would visit Pete's pirate ship. Since Paulie and Gina were spending a few days in town, they offered to take Violet with them to the hotel, so she could play with the kids and swim in the hotel's swimming pool.

Chirp. Carlita's phone chimed. It was Reese. She shifted Violet off her lap and headed to the balcony to talk. "I got your message."

"I chatted with the afternoon trolley driver, the one who filled in for my route including Walton Square. Hang on."

There was a moment of silence before Reese returned. "Anyhoo, he was asking how the wedding went and then mentioned a couple of passengers who were acting funny. He picked them up at your stop, right around the time of the wedding."

"Funny as in 'haha' funny?"

"No. Funny as in odd and acting suspiciously."

"Acting suspiciously?"

"Yes. Like very nervous. They were in a big hurry and asking unusual questions. Hang on again."

The line went silent. Reese returned. "Listen, I got too many people on this trolley to talk privately. Will you be riding the trolley in the morning?"

"Yep. I'll be on your first run."

"Perfect. We'll talk then. Gotta go."

Carlita thanked Reese and disconnected the line.

She stared at the phone, Megan's collapse weighing heavy on her mind. It was probably an unfortunate accident, so maybe she was reading too much into it.

Still, there was the break-in at the restaurant, hours before the wedding, not to mention the mysterious and headless cake topper. As far as Carlita knew, neither Tony nor Shelby had enemies in Savannah, but maybe someone was intent on ruining their wedding.

She ran inside to grab a piece of scrap paper and an ink pen. Mercedes was in the kitchen, pouring a glass of tea. "What are you doing?"

"Taking some notes. Reese called. She said the trolley driver who was running the Walton Square route earlier today, picked up a couple of riders who were acting suspiciously and thought it might mean something."

"Reese couldn't elaborate. I'm gonna talk to her first thing tomorrow morning." Carlita carried the pen and paper to the counter and began a bullet point list:

- Headless cake topper - in unmarked box.
- Break-in at the restaurant.
- Eddie shows up unexpectedly and uninvited.
- Vito sends bodyguards after threat to family.
- Trolley passengers - suspicious behavior.
- Megan Burelli's collapse during wedding.

She handed the list to Mercedes. "These can't all be coincidental."

Mercedes scanned the list and handed it back to her mother. "I think you're a little paranoid. Do you really believe Uncle Eddie is involved?"

"I'm not counting anyone out. I'll know more after I talk to Reese."

Rambo padded into the kitchen, looking for a treat. "How about a treat and a walk?" Carlita reached into the cupboard and pulled Rambo's box of special treats out. "Violet, do you want to give Rambo a treat?"

"Yes." The young girl bounced off the sofa and skipped into the kitchen. "What about Grayvie? He wants a treat, too."

"I'm sure Grayvie does." Carlita called for her cat, who lay curled up and napping on the dining room chair. He stalked into the kitchen and waited patiently for Violet to offer him a treat.

"How would you like to take Rambo for a walk?"

"Okay."

"I'll go with you," Mercedes said. "The fresh air will do me good."

"It's time to change out of your dress," Carlita told the child.

Violet gave Carlita a skulking look. She reluctantly carried her backpack to the bathroom to change.

"We'll wait for you in the hall." Carlita led Rambo out of the apartment.

Mercedes joined them. She scowled when she noticed Sam Ivey's apartment door was ajar. "He keeps his door open all of the time."

"So?" Carlita shrugged. "Does it matter?"

"Yes. It's weird. He's weird. He has very unusual habits, and it gives me the creeps."

Chapter 11

"Mercedes," Carlita chided. "Sam is a nice man. I don't know why you dislike him so much."

"You're blinded by his insincere niceness." Mercedes pulled her mother closer. "I think he's spying on us."

"And you think I'm being paranoid?" Carlita scoffed. "Maybe he's spying on you, keeping an eye out, so he can harass you."

"I wouldn't doubt it," Mercedes muttered. "Anyways, I think it's weird."

"I'm ready." Violet hopped into the hall.

"Let's go." Carlita and Rambo led the others to the bottom of the stairs and into the alley. "Which way?"

"I want to wave to the Waving Girl," Violet said. "Can we ride the free boat?"

Carlita lifted her eyes. Although the summer sun was starting to set, there was still enough time to visit the Waving Girl. If they hustled, they would be able to squeeze in a quick boat ride to Hutchinson Island and back.

She wasn't sure when Vinnie and Brittney were returning, but she didn't need to be around to let them in. She'd given Vinnie a key to the building and the efficiency. "I don't see why not."

"I guess we're going to Morrell Park," Carlita told her pooch.

Violet held tightly to Mercedes' hand as she chattered on about the Waving Girl, the ferry and how she couldn't wait to go swimming in the hotel's pool.

Carlita was careful not to mention Shelby or Tony, thinking she might be sad her mother was gone. Violet was the one who brought her up. "Mommy and Tony are going to bring me a surprise."

"They are?" Mercedes asked. "What kind of surprise?"

"I don't know. A good one," Violet assured them. "But only if I'm a good girl."

When they reached the park, they made a beeline for the statue. Violet and Rambo made a game of running circles around the Waving Girl.

Carlita and her daughter basked in the mild evening temperatures as they sat on a nearby bench to watch.

Rambo was the first to call it quits. He plopped down at Carlita's feet and began panting.

"You wore poor Rambo out. Shall we head to the ferry?" Carlita pointed to the river. "I see it coming now. If we hurry, we can catch this one."

The trio and Rambo cut across the lawn and joined the long line of passengers waiting to board. The free ferry was the fastest way for Savannah visitors to reach Hutchinson Island. Guests who were staying at the large, luxurious resort used it, as well as others who planned to visit the convention center.

They were among the last to board and the only seats left were in the back. Violet sat near the window and peered out while Rambo settled in at Carlita's feet.

It was a quick ride across the river. After arriving, they waited until the other passengers got off before making their way up the ramp.

There wasn't much to do near the dock, other than walk around the convention center and the hotel grounds. The trio looped around the hotel and then returned to the boarding area to wait for the next ferry.

After finishing their ferry ride, they circled Walton Square, passing by the Book Nook, Colby's Corner Store and finally, the Shades of Ink tattoo shop.

"Maybe I should get a tattoo," Mercedes said.

"I want a tattoo," Violet said.

"It hurts...a lot," Carlita told her. "It's like a thousand bee stings."

Violet's eyes grew round as saucers. "I never want a tattoo."

"That's what I thought."

When they reached the apartment, Carlita found a note from Vinnie, telling them Brittney was tired and they'd gone to bed early but promised they would see them in the morning.

"I guess we're on our own." Carlita crumpled the note. "Leftovers it is, and we have plenty."

While they ate, they chatted about the pirate adventure.

"I gotta be up early to catch the seven o'clock trolley," Carlita reminded her daughter.

"Violet can stay here with me since you've got some errands to run," Mercedes said. "I thought I would get up kinda early, to check on Josh and the pawnshop. Violet can go with me."

"Thanks. I shouldn't be too long," Carlita glanced at Violet, who was having a hard time keeping her eyes open. "It's getting late. Time for us to hit the hay."

"I'm not tired," Violet whined.

"But Nana and Aunt Mercedes are. So is Rambo." Carlita pointed to the sleeping dog. "We have a busy day tomorrow."

*****

Carlita woke early the next morning. She was careful not to wake Violet, who was sleeping on a cot in the corner, as she slipped out of bed to get ready.

The skies were still dark as she crossed the street to the trolley stop. Thankfully, there was only a short wait before Reese, and the Big Peach stopped to pick her up.

"You're right on time." Carlita struggled to carry her bulky box up the narrow steps.

"For heaven's sake. What have you got inside there? An elephant?"

"Decorations I rented from Savannah Rental over on the other side of City Market. I need to drop them off early. I've got a full day today." Carlita told her friend they were sailing on board The Flying Gunner for the Pirates in Peril show.

"I heard it's a great show," Reese said. "Pirate Pete has really outdone himself. I plan to go one of these days. Not today, though. I'm pulling a full shift."

"Because you took time off yesterday for the wedding?"

"Yep, and it was worth every minute of it. The food was delicious, the wedding beautiful. You have some swell kids, Carlita."

"Thank you. They are good kids. Shelby is a wonderful addition to the family." Carlita grew silent as she thought about her new daughter-in-law, a small niggle of concern in the back of her mind over Shelby's recent health issues.

Reese interrupted her thoughts. "I polished off the leftovers you gave me last night. It's a shame there weren't any chicken parmesan sticks left. They were delicious."

"The parmesan sticks were one of the favorites," Carlita said. "They're not on Ravello's menu. With so many people raving about them, maybe I should add them."

"Definitely. They would sell like hotcakes."

The trolley rolled to a stop, and the Big Peach picked up a few more early morning passengers. Reese greeted them by name.

Carlita waited until they were on their way again. "On the phone yesterday, you told me the trolley driver who filled in for you during the wedding mentioned that he picked up a couple of interesting riders."

"Yes. Jim said he picked them up at your stop. Sketchy is what he called them. They weren't regulars. He'd never seen them before."

"I'm sure there are all kinds of interesting people who board the trolleys," Carlita pointed out.

"Yep. I can attest to that fact. We get 'em all of the time." Reese patted her jacket pocket. "Which is why I pack heat."

Carlita lifted a brow. "You...carry a handgun?"

"Close enough. It's a Voltek 650, one of the most powerful Taser guns on the market. Cost me a pretty penny. I haven't used it yet. Just knowing it's close by gives me peace of mind."

"I'll have to remember that. So the riders were acting suspiciously."

"Yep. They asked Jim a bunch of questions about Walton Square, the businesses in the area, if there was a lot of crime in Savannah."

"Maybe they were just making conversation."

"That's what I told Jim, and I probably would've thought the same thing. It was one of the last questions they asked before getting off that Jim found interesting."

Chapter 12

"They wanted to know where they could purchase a gun."

"A gun?"

"Right, and then they wanted to know how to get to the bus station."

"The question about purchasing a gun raises a few red flags, but the question about the bus station isn't particularly odd, I suppose." Carlita mulled over Reese's statement while she waited for passengers to exit and the next group to board the trolley. "Maybe they were in town on vacation or visiting friends and on their way out."

"I was thinking the same thing." Reese tapped the side of her forehead. "I was going down the same path until Jim asked them if they were in town visiting family or friends. One of them said 'yes.'

141

The other said 'no,' and then they gave conflicting stories."

"I wish we could figure out if they were guests at the wedding." Carlita stared out the window as they passed Colonial Park Cemetery. "Do you think Jim would remember what the couple looked like?"

"Maybe, maybe not." Reese glanced at Carlita in the rearview mirror. "The trolleys are equipped with surveillance cameras. Savannah Trolley installed 'em after a rider claimed they tripped over a rip in the aisle runner and sued. Now if we see anything suspicious, we start recording."

"Really?" Carlita clasped her hands. "So do you think he caught them on camera?"

"I already left a message to find out, but haven't heard back yet. He did say the couple was in a big hurry to get off the trolley. The woman forgot her small handbag."

"What was inside?"

"Jim said it contained some girlie stuff, but no ID. He turned it in to Buzz, our boss. I asked Buzz about it this morning. He said no one called to claim it yet. Course, if they were hightailing it out on the bus and there was nothing of value inside, I doubt they would come back for it."

"So there was no ID?"

"Nope. He made a point of reminding me employees are not allowed to rummage through the lost and found cabinet."

"Another company policy?"

"Yep. Could be clues inside the bag. Now, all we gotta do is figure out a way to get our hands on it. We're here." The Big Peach shuddered to a halt at the City Market stop.

Carlita stood. "I have a few errands to run. I'll hop back on in about an hour or so."

Reese waited for Carlita and her box of goodies to squeeze down the narrow bus stairs. "In the meantime, I'll do some thinking on how we can get our hands on the handbag. Before I forget, Jim did mention one other thing about the couple."

"What's that?"

"The man was carrying a purple camo backpack. He almost left it behind, too. Jim tried to hand it to him. The man snatched it up like he didn't want Jim to get too close to it."

"Maybe he was on a gun-buying spree, and there were weapons stashed inside."

"I dunno," Reese shrugged.

"Thanks, Reese," Carlita paused when she reached the bottom. "You're a good friend."

"So are you, Carlita. I hate to see bad things happen to good people." Reese shut the Big Peach's door, and the trolley rumbled off.

Thankfully, the rental store was a short walk from the trolley stop. Carlita returned the rented items and then headed toward the bank to take care of the pawnshop's weekend deposits.

After finishing her transactions, she headed to a local coffee shop she'd stumbled upon during her last visit to the City Market. She perused the display case before purchasing a baker's dozen of donuts, figuring by the time she got home, Mercedes and Violet would be awake and hungry.

Carlita consulted her watch. There was still plenty of time before the Big Peach circled back around, so she wandered to Stalwart Street and to the Savannah Architectural Society's office to see if her friend, Glenda, was around.

The bell chimed as Carlita stepped inside.

She spied Glenda talking to someone standing at the counter. The woman's nasally voice was easily recognizable.

Carlita tiptoed across the room and tapped Elvira on the shoulder. "What are you doing here? Trying to get your old job back?"

"We wouldn't hire Elvira back if she was the last person in Savannah looking for a job," Glenda laughed.

"Very funny," Elvira huffed. "You wish I would come back to this dump and do your dirty work."

"Elvira." Glenda feigned surprise. "You took great pleasure in telling residents and business owners what they could and couldn't do."

"Yeah, well most of them were morons. I saved Savannah from half a dozen hideous paint jobs."

Carlita pointed to a pile of papers. "What are those?"

"Nothing." Elvira snatched the papers off the counter.

"Elvira is filling out an application to add an arch to the front entrance of her apartment building."

"How can you do that?" Carlita asked. "It isn't even your building."

"It will be within a day or so," Glenda said. "When is the closing again?"

"Big mouth." Elvira scowled at Glenda.

"You...you're buying the building behind me?" After moving out of Carlita's rental unit, Elvira had taken up residence in the lower level of the vacant building directly behind hers.

"I was gonna surprise you."

"More like shock. I didn't know the building was for sale."

"It wasn't. I made Davis an offer he couldn't refuse. The closing is tomorrow."

"Where did you get the money? Did you rob a bank?" Carlita teased.

"No. Dernice squirreled away some money she got from a motorcycle injury lawsuit."

"Oh no." A concerned expression crossed Carlita's face.

"She's okay now, although she's got a slight limp when she walks."

"I never noticed. What happened?"

"A car carrier cut her off on the Ventura Freeway. She jerked the handlebars trying to get out of his way and slid into a concrete barrier. Lucky for her, she wasn't going fast and was wearing a helmet. The lawyers came out in droves, offering to handle her case and wanting to sue. She hired a top-notch firm, but they charged her an arm and a leg to handle the case. She got a big payout, although it was peanuts compared to the lawyers."

Elvira tapped the top of her head with her knuckles. "I think the accident rattled her brain. She has some very strange ideas bouncing around in there."

"No." Carlita shook her head. "I don't think the accident messed with her head. I think it's a hereditary trait."

"What's that supposed to mean?" Elvira frowned.

148

"But she still walked away with money," Glenda interrupted.

"Yep. In the high six figures, after the lawyer's cut. The carrier was hauling racecars. During the negotiations, Dernice's lawyer hammered out a deal for a lifetime of racecar passes. I sweetened my offer to Davis with a year of racecar passes that Dernice will never use."

"You're saying the passes sealed the deal?"

"Yep. He's in hog heaven. Course Dernice could care less about car racing. Now if it was Harley racing? She would've been all over that."

"Aren't you the savvy business negotiator," Carlita teased.

"You have to be in the security and surveillance business. Competition is tough." Elvira turned to Glenda. "So are you gonna approve the arch or do I have to go over your head?"

"You know the drill, Elvira. It's policy to submit all requests to the committee. Before I do, I'll need a sketch of the design, along with actual dimensions."

"I figured you might make an exception since I'm a former employee." Elvira folded her papers and shoved them in her pocket.

"Nope. I'm not bending the rules."

"Fine. I'll get them to you this afternoon. I gotta get going. The wedding security detail yesterday set me back on my errands."

"It was a beautiful wedding," Glenda smiled at Carlita. "Thank you for inviting Mark and me."

"You're welcome. I meant to ask you, Elvira...were there many people trying to get inside the restaurant who weren't wedding guests?"

"There were a few. I told them you were opening on Friday and yesterday was a private event, like you wanted me to say."

"You stayed at the front entrance during the entire event."

"Yep." She nodded. "Except for a couple of bathroom breaks when Dernice covered for me."

"While you were there, did you happen to notice a couple, a man and a woman, who left the wedding reception early and boarded the trolley? It would have been after the cocktail hour, but I think it was before dinner."

"I saw a lot of people. Like I said, most of them were wedding guests." Elvira rubbed her chin thoughtfully. "Yeah. Now that you mention it, there was a couple who looked kinda suspicious. I figured they weren't locals since most locals are familiar with the trolley schedule."

"So you think they may have been tourists?"

"They definitely weren't wedding guests because they were wearing shorts and sandals. It was a man and woman, younger." Elvira closed her eyes. "Yep. They waited for the trolley for a good half an hour.

The woman kept looking over my way. I don't remember talking to them, and neither tried to get inside the restaurant."

"Can you describe them?"

Elvira's eyes flew open. "I just told you. Younger, wearing casual summer clothes and sandals."

Carlita forced her voice to remain even. "But nothing stood out as unusual or extraordinary."

"Nope. Both were Caucasian, medium height; sandy brown hair for him and lighter colored hair for her. I remember admiring the man's slick backpack."

Finally…Carlita might be onto something. "What about his backpack?"

"It was camo purple, my favorite color."

Chapter 13

"Camo purple," Carlita repeated. "You're sure."

"Positive. Like I said, I thought it was pretty cool and of course, my favorite color." Elvira glanced at her watch. "I better get going if I want to catch a trolley other than evil Reese's trolley."

"You wouldn't have a problem with Reese if you stopped harassing her riders and trying to sneak on without paying."

"She's lying," Elvira insisted. "I paid. She's just getting senile and forgets."

"What about harassing the other riders?"

"So I asked a coupla riders a coupla questions. She has it in for me. Reese is nothing but a troll who drives an ugly peach trolley."

"The Big Peach," Carlita corrected.

"Big and ugly." Elvira marched to the door. "Hey, what was inside the mysterious box I picked up yesterday morning?"

"It was a...cake topper." Carlita left off the part about it being headless. The less Elvira knew the better. "I still don't know who sent it."

"If I get a chance, I'll take a look at my surveillance camera. It's motion sensitive. It would've picked up anyone dropping it off in the alley."

"That would be great. How much will it cost me?"

"We're still on for my business card display inside your restaurant?"

"Of course. A deal is a deal."

"Then it won't cost you. Unless I think of something good." Elvira slipped out of the building. She walked past the front picture window and disappeared from sight.

"She's a trip."

"She is," Glenda agreed. "And just think - she's going to be your forever neighbor."

"That's not funny."

"I heard the young woman who collapsed at the wedding is in serious condition."

Carlita sobered. "Yes. I haven't gotten an update today. According to Elvira's secret source, she collapsed after ingesting a toxic substance."

Glenda gasped. "From your food?"

"I hope not, but it could be." Carlita sighed heavily. "I'm waiting to hear back from Officer Clousen."

"But you're thinking it might be something else?" Glenda asked.

"Maybe." Carlita eyed her friend, wondering how much she should share. "There were a couple of suspicious incidents before the wedding that make me wonder."

"A threat?"

"It depends on whether you would classify receiving a headless cake topper a threat."

Glenda's hand flew to her mouth. "And it was sitting on your back step before the wedding?"

"Yep. It was inside the unmarked package Elvira picked up. Someone also broke into the restaurant, busting through the back door, but they didn't take anything."

"How frightening," Glenda murmured. "Have you mentioned it to the authorities?"

"Not yet. I figured I would wait until I heard from them first." Carlita kept quiet about her suspicions the incidents might have involved the "family."

What if she'd unwittingly hired a worker or workers whose intent was to take out Brittney or Vinnie? She barely knew her new kitchen crew, having put Dominic in charge of hiring them.

"Are you okay?" Glenda asked. "You turned white as a ghost."

"I...I think I'm tired. I should head back to the trolley stop. Reese will be along shortly to pick me up."

"Keep your chin up," Glenda said. "I'm sure the authorities will find out the young woman's collapse was unrelated to the wedding."

Carlita nodded absentmindedly. "Thanks. I'll see you later." She wandered back to the stop, her head spinning. She needed to get her hands on a picture of the mysterious trolley riders with the purple camo backpack. Perhaps Reese had come up with an idea.

The Big Peach rounded the corner and pulled up to the curb.

"Hey." Reese looked as if she were about to explode into a million tiny pieces as she waved at Carlita.

"You thought of something."

"You betcha." Reese waited until the passengers boarded and they were on their way. "I'm going to tell Buzz that you're missing a small handbag, similar to the one the woman left on the trolley."

"So you're going to tell your boss you think the woman stole it from me?"

"Sure. I mean, Jim already mentioned they were acting suspiciously. You're an area business owner. Buzz won't even question it. He's a big suck up anyways."

Reese continued. "I was going to talk to him after my shift ends, but I came up with an even better idea. I think you should come with me."

Carlita mulled over Reese's idea. She wanted to have a look inside the handbag. Perhaps there was some sort of clue. "I...I'm not good at lying, but I suppose it's worth a try."

"Perfect. I'll pick you up at five-fifty."

"I ran into Elvira in the Savannah Architectural Society office. She made me wonder if there's a possibility I hired the two people on the trolley and they're the ones who contaminated the food."

"But why?"

"I have a few theories. It's still too early to start pointing fingers." How could Carlita tell her new friend that her family, and even her eldest son, had ties to the mob?

When they reached Walton Square, Carlita gathered her things and hopped off. "I'll see you later."

"You got it. This is exciting," Reese beamed. "I had a feeling about you when I met you."

"That I was trouble?"

"No, that you're special."

Carlita shook her head. "I'm special all right. Specially cursed."

She trudged across the street to the pawnshop to check on Josh and the other employee, who had just arrived.

After a brief conversation, she left a few glazed donuts behind and climbed the stairs to the apartment.

When she got to the top, Carlita noticed Sam's apartment door was ajar, and she grinned. Maybe he was spying on them. Or more specifically, keeping an eye out for Mercedes.

She stepped inside the apartment and found Violet on the sofa, watching television. Mercedes was sitting at her desk in the dining room.

"I brought breakfast." Carlita waved the bag of donuts.

"We already munched on a couple of cookies," Mercedes said. "We also ate a bowl of cereal."

"I'm still hungry." Violet slid off the sofa. "Chocolate donuts are my favorite."

"I thought Nonna's Italian cookies were your favorite," Carlita teased. "I picked out a bunch of different kinds and a special one for you. It has chocolate frosting and sprinkles."

"Yay!" Violet clapped her hands. "I love chocolate and sprinkles."

"Me, too." Carlita placed the donuts on the table and walked into the kitchen.

"The coffee is still warm," Mercedes said.

"Thanks." Carlita poured a cup. "What are you doing?"

"I'm going over the tenant applications. I wish I had as much luck finding prospective tenants as you were at finding restaurant workers."

"I don't know if I did that great of a job. Wait'll you hear this." Carlita helped Violet with her donut and carried it to the living room coffee table. "Make sure Rambo and Grayvie don't eat your donut. They can't have donuts."

"I know." Violet's head bobbed up and down. "Only special treats when you tell me."

"Good girl." Carlita patted her head and returned to the dining room. She briefly told her daughter about the handbag, the purple camo backpack and the suspicious behavior of the couple on the trolley. "Reese has a plan to have a look inside the forgotten handbag."

"There's something else." Carlita lowered her voice. "If the woman was poisoned, I'm seriously thinking it would have to have been an inside job."

"Inside?" Mercedes shook her head. "How? By one of our kitchen crew?"

"Think about it. I don't know them. They're all new. Who's to say that whoever has it in for Vito's family didn't send someone down here as a plant, to taint the appetizers and take Brittney out?"

"You think someone up north is that smart? Aren't mobsters more likely to shoot now and shoot later? Don't bother with trying to cover up?"

"Yeah, but maybe there's another reason. I need to take a closer look at the employee applications. I gotta run next door to get them. They're in the filing cabinet."

"I'll go with you," Mercedes offered. "I think it's best if we not go over there alone, especially with Tony and Shelby on their honeymoon and their upstairs apartment empty. You never know if someone will try to break in again."

"True." Carlita waited for Violet to finish her donut before shooing her into the bedroom to get dressed.

Mercedes threw on some clothes and the trio, along with Rambo, headed down the alley to the back entrance of the restaurant.

Carlita held the door and motioned them inside. The smell of fresh garlic and Italian spices lingered in the air.

"It smells delish in here." Mercedes sniffed appreciatively.

"It stinks." Violet wrinkled her nose. "Like yucky stuff."

"You have to be a grown up to appreciate Italian smells." Carlita made her way to the filing cabinet in the corner. She pulled out the stack of employee file folders and handed half to her daughter. "I have no idea what to look for."

"Me neither." Mercedes carried her stack to the counter and rifled through them. She skimmed through the names and addresses, focusing her attention on the previous employers and the locations.

Nothing stood out as a clue. It wasn't until she began going over the fourth one, something caught Mercedes' eye. "Hey, Ma. I think I might've found something."

Chapter 14

Carlita dropped the folder she was holding. "What did you find?"

"Check out this employee's previous work history."

Carlita adjusted her reading glasses and studied the section. "Duane Sorensen. He just moved to Savannah."

"But above that."

"He worked in..."

"New York." Mercedes finished her mother's sentence. "What if he was the plant? Do you recall what he looked like?"

"Not off the top of my head. I would have to find out if he was scheduled to work during the wedding. We can figure that out real quick." Carlita reached into the cabinet and pulled out her handwritten notes, including a list of employees who were working the wedding.

Her pulse ticked up a notch when she spotted his name. "Yes. As a matter of fact, he was working."

"But you met all of the employees, right?"

"Right," Carlita confirmed. "Dominic handled the hiring process, but I was the final say in the hires. It's possible Dominic let him leave early if he didn't need all of the employees sticking around after dinner."

"True. It could be a clue if he did leave before the reception ended."

Carlita set a wiggling Violet on the floor. "I'm going to call Officer Clousen and get to the bottom of this. Surely, by now he has a better idea of what happened to Megan Burelli."

"Let's take the employee folders and wedding planner back to the apartment," Mercedes said. "We might want to look at the files again later."

Carlita handed the file folders to her daughter and then followed Violet and Mercedes out the back door. They circled the block to give Rambo a chance to stretch his legs before returning to the apartment.

"I'll call the officer right now." Carlita dialed the number Clousen had given her and was surprised when he picked up.

"Officer Clousen speaking."

"Officer Clousen, this is Carlita Garlucci. We met yesterday in my courtyard when Ms. Burelli collapsed and was taken to the local hospital."

"Yes. Mrs. Garlucci. You were on my list to call today. I spoke with Ms. Burelli's companion. She explained her friend's initial symptoms, before collapsing. They match those of someone who ingested a substance causing life-threatening conditions."

The officer went on to explain he was speaking off the record and until the doctors knew more, the cause of her collapse was still officially undetermined.

"Thank you for the update. If I think of anything that can add to the investigation, I'll be sure to let you know." Carlita thanked the officer a second time and ended the call.

"Why didn't you tell him about the mysterious package?" Mercedes asked.

"Because it may be nothing, although it is beginning to look as if Megan Burelli consumed a tainted food substance, at the pre-dinner cocktail party no less." Carlita motioned Mercedes into the kitchen. "He would think I was nuts if I told him someone sent us a headless groom."

"If he believes Megan was poisoned, he'll be around soon enough," Mercedes predicted. "I'm sure he would be interested to know someone broke into the restaurant yesterday morning."

"True, but they didn't take anything. There's still the off chance the headless groom, the break-in and

Megan's incident is unrelated." At least Carlita was trying to convince herself of that.

First, she needed to find out what the mysterious couple who boarded the trolley in Walton Square yesterday looked like.

Violet skipped into the kitchen, smears of chocolate on her cheek and upper lip.

"Have you had chocolate on your face this whole time?" Carlita chuckled. "We need to wipe your face."

Violet licked her lips. "Is it gone?"

"No." Carlita led the young child into the bathroom as someone knocked on the door.

"I'll get it," Mercedes said. "It's probably Vinnie."

Carlita heard her son's voice and the tinkle of Brittney's laughter coming from the living room. They finished cleaning up, and Carlita and Violet joined them.

"Hello, Son." Carlita gave her son a quick hug and then hugged Brittney. "Did you sleep well?"

"Like a baby. We figured we'd swing by before heading to the stores to shoe shop," Vinnie said. "I thought maybe Mercedes would like to take my place," he hinted.

"No. We're going to meet Paulie and his family for the Pirates in Peril pirate show. Ma and I have been itching to see it."

"Are you sure?"

"Stop trying to weasel your way out of shopping." Brittney punched her husband's arm playfully. "It will be fun."

"Right."

"How was your dinner with Uncle Eddie and Aunt Anjelica?" Carlita asked. "I figured they would stop by to say good-bye."

"I thought they were gonna, too, but Uncle Eddie said they needed to get going. They wrapped up their small business matter here and were heading back. They told us they'd catch up with you next time they were down this way."

"They seemed in a big hurry to leave town." Brittney turned to Vinnie. "Don't you think your aunt and uncle seemed like they couldn't wait to leave?"

"Yeah, but then that's Uncle Eddie. He don't sit still for too long."

"Have you eaten yet?" Carlita asked. "I picked up some donuts over in the City Market this morning. The Bavarian Kreme donuts are delicious. They melt in your mouth."

"No thanks." Brittney made a face. "The thought of sugary foods this early makes me want to throw up."

"I'll eat her donut," Violet offered.

"No you won't," Carlita laughed. "You've already eaten enough sweets this morning."

Violet made a pouting face.

"We'll grab a bite to eat on our way to the mall," Vinnie said. "Thanks for the offer."

They chatted for a few more minutes before Vinnie stood. "We better get going. I have a feeling it's gonna be a long day." He gave his wife a hand up, and they wandered to the front door.

Carlita followed them into the hall.

Mercedes trailed behind. "Ugh."

"What?"

"Over there." Mercedes pointed to Sam's apartment door, still ajar. "I told you."

"That's silly," Carlita said. "Sam is not spying on us."

"Sam Ivey, your new tenant?" Vinnie asked.

"Yes. Mercedes is convinced that he's spying on us."

"Maybe he's got the hots for you," Vinnie teased. "He wants to keep an eye out."

Mercedes' face turned bright red. "He does not have the hots for me. We can't stand each other."

"Ah." A slow smile crept across her brother's face. "Now I get it."

"You do not." Mercedes marched into the apartment and slammed the door behind her.

"Yeah, there's definitely some interest," Vinnie said.

"You noticed too." Carlita changed the subject. "So what time do you think you'll be back for dinner?"

"How 'bout seven-thirty?"

After agreeing on the time, Carlita and Violet made their way back inside.

Mercedes was in her room, the door closed. Carlita tapped on the outside. It flew open, and she stumbled back, almost tripping on Violet who was directly behind her. "I hate it when you do that."

"Sorry, Violet," Mercedes apologized.

"That wasn't nice."

"I said I was sorry."

"I'm not talking about scaring us. I'm talking about you getting bent out of shape because of Sam Ivey and his apartment door."

"He just gets on my nerves." Mercedes glanced over her shoulder. "I think I'll work on my book for a while before getting ready for our pirate adventure."

"Violet and I will find something to entertain ourselves."

"I'm going swimming later," Violet said.

"Yes. And you're still going to spend the night with your new cousins Noel, Gracie and PJ."

"Yep." Violet nodded. "But first I want to color a picture."

Mercedes returned to her computer and Carlita and Violet spent the rest of the morning coloring pictures. She colored one for her mother, one for Mercedes and one for Carlita.

Lunchtime consisted of a sandwich and chips. After cleaning up, the trio walked to the river, where The Flying Gunner was docked.

Mercedes, Violet and Carlita stood off to the side, waiting for Paulie and his family. They appeared a short time later and then everyone joined the line with Carlita leading the way.

She smiled at the woman behind the ticket counter. "Hello. I don't have a reservation. My name is Carlita Garlucci. Pirate Pete is expecting me and my family."

"Yes. Mrs. Garlucci. Pete said you would be joining us." The girl, *Isla*, according to her nametag, counted the children. "Perfect, we have all four junior pirates." She reached into the cabinet and pulled out four paper pirate hats and four plastic swords.

"Pete picked out your pirate names ahead of time." Isla eyed the side of the first pirate hat. "Which one of you is Gracie?"

"Me." Gracie raised her hand.

"You're now Cap'n Gracie Roughknuckles." Gracie giggled as Isla placed the pirate hat on top of her head. "Where's Violet?"

"Here." Violet pranced forward. "I'm Violet."

"Not anymore. Pirate Pete dubbed you Churnin' Violet Dagger." Isla placed the pirate hat on Violet's head. "You must be PJ." She pointed to Carlita's grandson.

"Yep."

"You're now PJ the Jolly Pirate." Isla slid the hat on PJ's head and smiled at Noel. "Miss Noel." She waved the paper pirate hat. "Pirate Pete picked the perfect name for you."

Noel inched forward, her eyes 'round as saucers. "He did?"

"Yes." Isla nodded solemnly.

"You're Cap'n Shark Tooth Noel." Noel grinned as Isla placed the hat on her head.

Isla handed each of the children a plastic sword, but first made them promise not to stab one another and then motioned the Garlucci family on board.

They passed by Gunner, who was in his cage and stationed near the ramp greeting the guests. "Aye, matey. The Flying Gunner is getting ready to set sail."

"This is Gunner," Violet told the other children. "He's funny."

"Gunner is handsome," the parrot squawked.

"Hello, Gunner," Carlita said. "It's going to be a beautiful day to walk the plank."

Gunner strutted along his perch. "Time to walk the plank."

It had been weeks since the last time Carlita boarded The Flying Gunner to assist Pete in interviewing potential employees. It looked different now. The ship sported a spacious snack bar and comfy sofa seating. Eerie lanterns glowed green and orange.

"This looks different," Mercedes said. "I love the new look."

"Me, too."

They explored the lower deck before heading upstairs to the open deck.

Carlita heard Pirate Pete's booming voice echo from the bow of the ship. "And, then I said to my first mate, Sully, we be needin' to fire a shot across the bow."

The children gathered around Pirate Pete. He was dressed in full pirate garb, from the plumed pirate hat perched atop his head, to his fitted puffy pirate shirt all the way down to his shiny black pirate breeches. A black patch covered his right eye.

"Ah, more mates for our sword fight." Pete winked at Carlita. "And what about you, pretty lady?" he teased.

"I think I'll hang out on the sidelines," Carlita chuckled.

Another garbed pirate tapped the tip of his sword on Pete's shoulder. "You be looking for me?"

"Ahh...it's the dastardly Johnny Dud." Pete chased the pirate to a stack of towering wooden boxes as the men dueled with their swords.

Carlita's grandchildren stood nearby, entranced by the sword fight. The sword fight ended with the heroic Pirate Pete capturing Johnny Dud.

The pirate ship set sail a short time later, cruising along the riverfront, past the Waving Girl landing and the ferry.

They sailed all the way to Fort Jackson before turning around and starting the return trip to Gunner's Landing, the ship's slip.

While the children played pirates, the adults munched on popcorn and sipped sodas. The host of activities included a treasure hunt, followed by a water gun shootout.

After the water gun battle, the children joined their parents for popsicles and snow cones.

All too soon, the exciting pirate adventure ended.

Pirate Pete and his merry band of buccaneers lined the gangway, thanking the guests for joining them as they disembarked. They were also handing out discount coupons to Pete's restaurant, The Pirate House.

Pete caught Carlita's eye and waved her off to the side. "Any news on your wedding guest's condition?"

"Yes." Carlita motioned to Paulie. "I'll be right with you."

Mercedes slipped past her brother and joined her mother and Pete. "We had an awesome pirate adventure."

"Thank you, Mercedes. I was askin' your mother about the condition of your wedding guest."

"She's in intensive care. Elvira claims she heard it was food poisoning."

"Shiver me timbers." Pete placed a light hand on his scabbard. "Are they thinking it was something she ate at the reception?"

"It's possible. We're still waiting on the official word."

Pete rubbed his beard thoughtfully. "I was gonna mention yesterday, an odd situation that happened during the wedding."

Chapter 15

Pete continued. "I stopped by your kitchen to compliment your staff on the bang up job they did on the food. After I got done, I stepped out back to make a quick call to check on the early pirate ship run."

"Elvira's sister, Dernice, was in the alley and she gave you a hard time," Carlita guessed.

"No. Dernice wasn't around. There was a coupla people standing near the dumpster, a man and a woman. The woman was crying. I asked if everything was okay. The man, the one wearing a uniform, assured me that they were fine."

"A uniform?"

"Yes. It looked like one of your restaurant uniforms. He whispered something in the woman's ear. The man grabbed their stuff, and they took off."

Carlita's heart began to pound. "What kind of stuff?"

"A purple backpack."

"Was it purple camo?"

Pete nodded. "You know who I'm talkin' about?"

"I think I do. The afternoon trolley driver, Jim, may have seen the same couple. He told Reese they were acting suspiciously. Do you think you'd be able to recognize the couple if you saw them again?"

"Yes. Most definitely."

Carlita had a sudden thought. "Did they talk funny?"

"Funny?"

"Like us...like they were from New York." Carlita thought of the threat to Vito's family. Was it possible Louie sent a couple of his soldiers to Savannah? They joined Carlita's restaurant staff with a plan to murder Vito's daughter...or even Vinnie.

"No, but then they weren't really talkin'." Pete shook his head.

One of the "pirates" joined them. "Sorry to interrupt, Pete. We got a guest inquiring about a group cruise."

"I'll let you go," Carlita said. "Thank you for the information and for giving all of us a wonderful pirate adventure. We enjoyed it immensely."

"I'm glad you and your family had a good time." Pete pressed the palm of his hand to his chest. "It warms the cockles of my black heart."

Mercedes waited until Pete walked away. "I think we're finally onto something. What if someone or some-ones managed to infiltrate our staff with the sole purpose of murdering Brittney?"

"There's one way we can find out. We'll call the cell phone number that's in the employee's file. What was his name?"

"Duane something. It would still take a couple of people to pull off an inside job," Mercedes said.

"There would need to be one who was working the crowd with trays of appetizers and drinks. A second would have to be behind the scenes, in the kitchen, tampering with the appetizers or drinks."

"The first thing we're gonna do when we get home is call Duane Sorensen's cell phone. I'll think of what to say on the way."

Mother and daughter joined Paulie and his crew, who were standing near the railing, tossing pieces of leftover popcorn in the water for the birds.

Carlita held up Violet's Elsa and Anna backpack. "Are you still going with Uncle Paulie and Aunt Gina to the hotel pool?"

"Yes." Violet took the backpack from Carlita. "Are you going, too?"

"I'm afraid not. Nana and Mercedes have some things to take care of at home."

Violet's lip quivered, and Carlita thought she might start to cry.

She knelt down next to the young girl. "I have an errand to run a little later. Why don't I stop by the hotel to check on you? You can let me know if you want to spend the night with your new cousins, or if you want to come home with Nana."

"Okay." Violet nodded solemnly.

Gracie slipped her small hand into Violet's hand. "It will be okay. Mommy said if we're good, we get to have ice cream later."

Touched by her granddaughter's tender heart, Carlita wrapped one arm around Gracie and the other around Violet. "I'm sure you're going to have so much fun, you won't remember Nana Banana."

"Let's go." Gina and Paulie herded the children down the sidewalk, toward the riverfront district and their hotel.

Mercedes tugged on her mother's arm as Carlita watched Violet leave with the others. "C'mon. Violet will be fine."

"But she's missing her mother," Carlita said. "I don't want her to feel like I'm abandoning her."

"She's going to have a ball. You worry too much." Mercedes linked arms with her mother, and they began walking in the opposite direction. "Like you said, you'll be checking on her later."

"True."

"And we have some sleuthing to do. First, we're going to track down Duane what's-his-name's cell phone number."

Mercedes abruptly stopped. "Ma."

"What?"

"The video. Remember when Megan collapsed and you asked me to take a quick video of the courtyard?"

"Yes. I remember now. Do you still have it?"

Mercedes plucked her cell phone from her back pocket and scrolled through the screen. "Yep."

Carlita peered over her daughter's shoulder, and they watched the short video. "I didn't catch anything."

"Me either. The screen is kinda small."

"We should definitely take a closer look. I'll send a copy to your email. When we get back to the apartment, we can check it out on the computer."

"Good idea."

Back home, the women stopped by the pawnshop to check on the employees. Josh, who was still working, assured them everything was running smoothly.

Carlita stepped into the back hall, and Mercedes closed the door behind them. "He's the pawnshop's best employee."

"Yes, he is," Carlita agreed.

They climbed the stairs to the upper hall, and Mercedes let out an irritated breath.

"What?"

"Over there." Mercedes frowned at Sam's door, still ajar. "Every time I'm in the hall, his door is ajar. I wonder if he quit his job."

"He's self-employed," Carlita pointed out. "Sam sets his own hours. Maybe he decided to take a day off."

"Yeah, well I'm sick of seeing his door open." Mercedes marched down the hall to Sam's door. She rapped hard, hard enough to push the door open. "Hello?"

"Mercedes." Carlita hurried after her.

"Who leaves their door open and unlocked when they're not home?"

"Can I help you?"

Mercedes nearly jumped out of her skin as Sam swung the door open, scaring her half to death.

"You!" Mercedes' eyes narrowed accusingly. "You did that on purpose."

"Did what?"

"You tried to scare me."

"No. I merely answered my door. You scared yourself."

Mercedes had certainly met her match. Carlita couldn't help it. She doubled over in gales of laughter.

"I did not. Ugh." Mercedes clenched her fists in frustration. "Why do you keep leaving your door open?"

Sam casually leaned his hip against the doorframe, peering down at Mercedes with a look of amusement on his face. "Is it bothering you?"

"Yes. It is bothering me. I feel like I'm being watched."

"I'm sorry you feel that way. I can assure you I have no desire to spy on you."

"Then do us all a favor and shut your dang door," she gritted out.

"Mercedes." Carlita grasped her daughter's arm. "Sam is entitled to leave his door open. As a matter of fact, he can run up and down the hall in his bathrobe if he wants. This is his home."

"Thank you, Carlita." Sam offered her a dazzling smile, which only seemed to enrage Mercedes.

"You're not helping, Ma."

"I apologize for distracting you, Mercedes. I never intended to be a distraction."

"You're not a distraction, attraction or whatever." Mercedes' rant made Sam smile even wider, and Carlita suspected he was enjoying the exchange immensely.

"I give up. Leave your door wide open. Run around in your underwear for all I care." She uttered something unintelligible under her breath and stomped inside their apartment, slamming the door behind her.

"She sure does like to slam doors," Sam commented. "Maybe that's why I leave my door open. I'm waiting for her to ask me if she can slam it."

Carlita tilted her head. "You would like that."

For once, Sam was at a loss for words.

"Ah. I see it in your eyes. You do like Mercedes." Carlita leaned in and whispered conspiratorially. "I think she likes you, too. She just has a funny way of showing it."

She winked at her tenant and then sauntered back to her own apartment.

Sam was still standing in his doorway when she stepped inside.

"Mercedes?"

"I'm in here."

Carlita wandered into the kitchen and found her daughter chowing down on a tub of chunky chocolate peanut butter ice cream. "Sam likes you. Really, he does."

"He has a funny way of showing it." Mercedes dropped the dirty spoon in the sink before placing the leftover ice cream back in the freezer. "I feel better already. It's time to get down to business."

Carlita grabbed the employee file folders and flipped through the applications. "I found Duane Sorensen's application and telephone number."

"I'll make the call." Mercedes reached for her phone.

Carlita rattled off the cell phone number while her daughter dialed.

What happened next, made them realize they might be onto something with the purple backpack-toting stranger and his companion.

Chapter 16

I'm sorry, but the number you have reached has been disconnected or is no longer in service.

Mercedes ended the call. "Well...that answers that. It appears Sorensen's cell phone has been disconnected."

"I say we try the other employee numbers while we're at it," Carlita said. "Just because Sorensen lived in New York doesn't mean he was the one in the alley, carrying a purple backpack and dressed in one of the restaurant's work uniforms."

"There's something else." She stared at her daughter thoughtfully. "Elvira mentioned the couple she saw waiting for the bus stop were both wearing casual clothing - not work uniforms."

"But they could've easily changed," Mercedes pointed out. "The backpack could've had a change of clothes."

"You're right." Carlita rubbed her hands together. "Let's finish going through the list."

All of the other numbers were legit except for one, which had also been disconnected.

"We'll add Rudy Swanson to the list of possible purple backpack employees, since his number has been disconnected, too." Carlita jotted his name on a sheet of paper. "Dominic might be able to help since he was in charge of the staff yesterday. He may know if an employee was acting suspiciously, and possibly even remember seeing the backpack."

"Good idea," Mercedes said. "We should take a closer look at my video of the courtyard yesterday, right after Megan collapsed." She sorted through the emails until she found the one with the video.

Carlita slipped her reading glasses on as Mercedes pressed the play button.

"You did a good job of getting everyone and everything," Carlita whispered.

"Thanks. I tried to pan slowly to get clear shots."

The beginning moments were of the courtyard entrance and Ricco. There were several guests milling about, all eyes focused off camera and Carlita guessed in the direction of poor Megan.

The video ended abruptly.

"Let's watch it again," Carlita said. "I didn't see anything."

Mercedes played the brief video a second time, starting with a view of the courtyard gate and Ricco, panning over the guests and ending near the courtyard wall where two of the servers huddled off to the side.

"Stop right there. Can we zoom in on the servers?"

"Yep." Mercedes tapped the mouse to enlarge the picture. "I don't recognize the servers, but I've only met them once, right after you and Dominic hired them."

"They look kinda familiar." Carlita forced herself to focus. One of the servers was balancing a tray of champagne flutes. The other was holding a tray of hors d' oeuvres. "Let's say...hypothetically speaking, one of the kitchen workers intentionally slipped something into one of the pre-dinner goodies. They then handed it off to their accomplice...a server, who then delivered it to the intended victim."

"But why Megan Burelli?"

"It wasn't supposed to be Megan Burelli. Go back to the footage of her."

Mercedes rewound to the part where Megan sat face down at the table, surrounded by her friend, Sam Ivey and Carlita.

"There." Carlita tapped the screen. "Megan is blonde, like Brittney. They look a lot alike. Even Ricco commented that at one point he thought

Vinnie was talking to Brittney. It would be fairly easy to confuse the two."

"I dunno." Mercedes frowned. "If this was a hit, wouldn't you want to make sure you took out the right person the first time?"

"They may have gotten confused; thinking the person Vinnie was with was his wife, Vito's daughter, the target. Oh my gosh." Carlita's mouth dropped open. "If my hunch is correct, they were both targets - Brittney and Vinnie. A double hit at the same time. I need to get to Vinnie."

Carlita's finger trembled as she dialed her son's cell phone. Vinnie picked up on the first ring. "Hey, Ma."

"Hey, Son. I'm sorry to bother you. I have a quick question."

"You're not bothering me. I'm hanging out, waiting for Brit to finish her shoe shopping. What's up?"

"Yesterday, during the wedding while you were out in the courtyard. You remember talking to the woman, Megan Burelli, briefly before Brittney came up and pulled you away."

"Do I ever," Vinnie groaned. "She thought the chick was flirting with me. I would never cheat on my Brit."

"I know, Son. I believe you. I'm not sure if I asked you this already, but while you were standing there, did the servers come around and ask you if you wanted an appetizer or a drink?"

"Yeah. They came around a bunch of times, offering food and champagne, especially the one with the tray of food. I figured she knew I was the owner's son and was trying to make a good impression."

"Did you eat the food?"

"No."

"I know this is an odd question, but do you remember if Megan Burelli ate the food?"

"Yeah. In fact, she told the server she would take my share of the chicken parmesan sticks. She ate them and seemed fine."

"But she ate them, and you didn't."

"Yep."

"That's helpful. I have another question. Do you think Megan Burelli resembles Brittney...from a distance or at a glance?"

There was a long pause. "I guess so. Don't tell Brit I said that, but yeah, I could see a resemblance." Vinnie cleared his throat. "You think someone was working on the inside, trying to poison Brit or me?"

"That's exactly what I think. I have other information, which leads me to believe that may have been the case. Vinnie, no one else got sick or poisoned by the food, just Megan, who you admitted resembles Brittney."

"You think Vito's inside info was correct. Esposito's people followed us to Savannah and infiltrated your work staff. They poisoned some of the food, and then tried to serve it to Brit and me? I don't think Louie's guys are that smart."

"They may be smarter than you think. I barely know the restaurant employees. On top of that, Vito sent his men to protect you. He must've believed there was a credible threat. It would almost have to be an inside job."

There was a muffled noise on the other end. "I hear you, Ma. Brit's done shopping. We can talk about this later."

"Be careful," Carlita warned. "You both may still be in danger."

"Right." Vinnie thanked his mother for her concern, and hung up the phone, promising they would be by later for dinner.

While Carlita talked, Mercedes printed off a screenshot of the two servers in the courtyard.

"Perfect." Carlita plucked the copy from the printer. "It's a little grainy, but I think you can make out enough of their features to identify them. Now all I have to do is show this to Pete to see if we have a match."

By the time they finished reviewing the employee records, it was time to head down to the trolley to meet Reese. "We better hurry or we're gonna be late."

Mercedes joined her mother at the door. "Do you have the print off of the two servers in the courtyard?"

"Right here." Carlita patted her purse. "We better get a move on or we're gonna miss the Big Peach."

Mercedes pulled the apartment door shut. "Good."

"Huh?"

"Sam finally shut his door." Mercedes nodded toward the end unit. "Maybe my calling him out did the trick, and he'll stop spying on us."

"Sam is not spying on us." Carlita rolled her eyes. "Or maybe he's spying on you. He's a real catch."

"Yuck," Mercedes snorted. "Then I hope someone else does the catching."

The women reached the trolley stop, moments before the Big Peach rounded the corner.

Reese tooted the horn and rolled to a stop. "Whew. What a crazy day. The Peach's lights went on the fritz again. I swear they're keeping tune to my CD player. Check this out."

She adjusted the volume, and *Jingle Bells* began to play, the trolley's interior lights keeping tune with the song. "See?"

"Christmas music in the middle of summer? Maybe there's a short." Carlita settled into her usual seat, directly behind Reese.

Mercedes took the seat opposite her mother. "I think it's cool. You should leave it that way."

"The riders seem to like it." Reese waited while more passengers hurried across the street, and boarded the trolley. They made their way to the back, leaving Carlita and Mercedes alone with Reese.

"I have some good news, and interesting developments," Carlita said.

"Pertaining to our investigation?" Reese asked.

"Yes. We might be onto something."

"I have some news too. Unfortunately, it's not good."

Chapter 17

"You were able to get your hands on the mysterious handbag, and it was empty," Carlita guessed.

"No. I'm good, but not that good," Reese said. "There's no video footage of the couple in question. I checked on my break."

"Crud. So that shoots down one of my ideas to link the mysterious trolley riders to possible restaurant workers."

"We need to go over our plan to convince Buzz to let us have a lookie inside the mysterious handbag," Reese said. "He may ask you to describe it. Buzz is kinda funny about the lost and found stuff."

Mercedes wrinkled her nose. "I see a big problem with that...we don't know anything about the handbag."

"You're wrong. Jim described it to me. It's small, gray and it has girlie stuff inside."

"What kind of girlie stuff?" Carlita asked.

"Well...that's where it gets a little tricky. When I asked Jim to elaborate on the contents, the only thing he could tell me is that it was small and gray and he *thinks* there was a bottle of hand sanitizer."

"Hand sanitizer," Mercedes repeated. "I think I can handle this."

"Better you than me," Carlita muttered.

"We're here."

Carlita and Mercedes waited near the front entrance while Reese drove the trolley around back to the parking garage. She joined them a short time later. "You ready for this?"

Mercedes sucked in a breath and nodded. "As ready as I'll ever be."

They followed Reese through the reception area and down a narrow hall, stopping in front of an open door. "Hey, Buzz."

"Reese. C'mon in," a gruff voice echoed out.

Carlita followed Reese into the office, and Mercedes brought up the rear.

"We're here to see if Mercedes can identify her missing handbag," Reese said.

"Yep." Buzz shoved his chair back and stood. "Before we do that, can you describe the handbag? We got a couple in the lost and found."

Mercedes gave her mother a quick glance. "Yes. It's small and gray. It's a spare I don't use often, that's probably why I accidentally left it on the trolley."

"I got two gray handbags. Can you describe it a little better?"

"No. I mean, it's a handbag, and it's gray."

Buzz eyed them suspiciously before opening the closet door. He pulled out two handbags and held them up.

Mercedes stared at them, unsure of which one to pick.

"It's that one." Reese lunged forward and attempted to snatch the bag he was holding in his left hand, but Buzz held tight, refusing to let go. "Hold your horses. Can you tell me what was inside?"

"I always carry lip balm and hand sanitizer."

"Anything else?" Buzz dangled the handbag in front of them.

"No." Mercedes frowned. "Like I said, I rarely use the handbag."

"Is this yours...or isn't it?" Buzz's eyes narrowed.

"It kind of looks like mine."

"Huh." Buzz reluctantly handed the bag to Mercedes.

She unzipped the top, stuck her hand inside and pulled out a container of dental floss. Next, she reached in and pulled out a small bottle of hand sanitizer.

Carlita's heart pounded loudly as Mercedes stuck her hand inside the bag a third time. She pulled out a pink stapler. "This...doesn't look familiar."

"So you're saying the bag isn't yours?" Buzz asked.

"I..." Mercedes reached in the bag again and felt around. "It's empty." She placed the items back inside and handed it to Buzz. "Nope. The bag isn't mine. It looks a lot like one that I have, but this isn't it."

"No kidding." Buzz took the bag, giving Mercedes an odd look.

"Mercedes has a lot of handbags," Carlita laughed. "Even I can't keep track of them."

Reese thanked her boss for showing them the handbag, and then quickly ushered her friends out of his office.

Mercedes waited until they were out of the building to speak. "I don't think your boss believed me."

"Can you blame him? You weren't even close on guessing the contents, except for the hand sanitizer," Carlita said.

"Yeah, but who carries dental floss, and a stapler around in their purse? No one. That's who."

"She has a point," Reese said. "At least he let her look inside."

Carlita motioned toward the trolley office. "Reese, what if you picked the wrong handbag? What if it was the other one?"

"No, I picked the right one. I forgot one minor detail Jim gave me. He said the handbag had a long strap. The other gray one had a short strap."

The trio made their way to the end of the street, circling back around the side, and to the front.

"It looks like we'll have to walk home."

"I have it covered. Our ride is parked over there, in the hotel parking garage." Reese pointed to a high rise-parking garage. "I gave the manager a complimentary trolley pass. In exchange, I get free parking."

"That's a nice perk," Carlita said.

The women walked toward the parking garage. "I don't do swaps with too many people. Frank was down on his luck at the time, pounding the pavement and looking for a job. When I found out, I gave him free rides around town during his job search."

"How thoughtful of you, Reese." Despite Reese's gift for gab, at times nearly nonstop, she had a heart of gold and was always willing to help a friend or even a stranger in need.

Carlita was indeed lucky to call Reese her friend. "Thank you for helping us. I'm sorry our fact finding mission was a bust."

There was a moment of silence, and Carlita could see Reese's wheels spinning. "At least you still have the video footage of the courtyard right after Megan's collapse. If I were you...not saying I am, but if I were you, I would have Pirate Pete take a look at it."

"We were thinking the same thing," Mercedes said. "He told Ma he thinks he would be able to identify the people he ran into in our alley."

"It's getting late. The kids are coming over for dinner. It will have to wait until tomorrow."

"Over here." Reese veered off the sidewalk and headed for the parking garage's side service door.

Flickering yellow bulbs hung from the concrete ceiling, casting creepy shadows inside the parking garage.

Mercedes shivered. "I don't think I would want to be wandering around in here by myself, especially after dark."

"This is the valet parking area, for employees only. It doesn't seem to bother Frank."

"It would make the perfect spot for a murder mystery," Carlita said.

"You're right, almost a little too perfect of a spot."

"Our ride is over there." The women crossed to the other side of the parking garage, to a four-wheel drive jeep parked in the corner.

Reese unlocked the doors and motioned for them to get in.

"I never would've pegged you for a four-wheel drive person," Carlita said.

Reese tossed her purse in the back seat and climbed in. "What did you think I would drive?"

"A trolley. Seriously," Carlita said. "I dunno. Maybe a four-door luxury sedan, something with plenty of room."

"I wouldn't be caught dead in a tin tank. Those are for mature adults or senior citizens."

"Then you'll never want to ride around in our car." Mercedes crawled into the back seat. "We have a Lincoln town car."

"No kidding. I never would've pegged *you* for driving a big tank like that."

"It was my husband, Vinnie's, car. Mercedes and I inherited it after his death."

Mercedes reached for the seatbelt. "We inherited it, and then we spent some fun-filled hours learning how to drive it."

Reese pulled her door shut and started the jeep. "I can't imagine it's much different than driving any other vehicle, except bigger."

"We didn't know how to drive," Carlita said.

Dumbfounded, Reese's jaw dropped. She stared at Carlita. "You didn't know how to drive...a car?"

"Nope. Vinnie always drove me around, or I took the bus. Mercedes had a driver's license, but rarely drove."

"We didn't have much use for it in New York," Mercedes explained.

"We lived a different life back then."

"I guess you don't need to drive much here in Savannah either," Reese said.

"Because we have a friend who drives the trolley and I can get wherever I need to go."

"But you do know how to drive now." Reese stopped at the stop sign before pulling onto the street.

"Yes. We both know how to drive, and open bank accounts and balance a checkbook," Carlita said. "Which comes in handy when you own several businesses."

"You mentioned before you lived a sheltered life in New York. I had no idea." Reese tapped the steering wheel. "Well, you got it all going on now and a mysterious poisoning to boot."

It didn't take long for them to get to the other side of town. Reese steered her jeep into the alley behind the apartment. "Am I gonna see you tomorrow?"

"I don't know." Carlita reached for the door handle. "Paulie and Gina will still be in town. I think Vinnie and Brittney are heading out in the morning, along with Vinnie's co-workers. Tony and Shelby will be back from their short honeymoon."

"We need to get with Pirate Pete," Mercedes reminded her mother.

"Yes, we do. If I don't see you tomorrow, I'm sure I'll see you on Tuesday." Carlita slid out of the jeep. "Thanks again for trying to help. You're a good friend Claryce...Reese, Magillicuddy."

"And so are you, Carlita Garlucci." Reese held up a hand. "I do have one more thing up my sleeve."

"Concerning our investigation?"

"Yep. I have a friend who happens to be a ticket agent for the bus station our two mysterious riders were asking about."

"You do? Can you ask your friend if she remembers seeing them?"

"I already have. I'm just waiting for a call back from Dixie, my friend."

Mercedes squeezed out of the back seat. "Do you need identification to buy a bus ticket?"

"It depends. Not if it's a local ticket used for riding around Savannah. If the person or persons were going out of state or out of the area, they would need a photo ID to buy a ticket."

"We may have a match and even a name." Carlita clasped her hands. "That would be awesome."

Mercedes smiled. "You sure do have connections."

"Friends with planes, trains and automobiles," Reese joked.

"And busses."

"I'll let you know as soon as I hear back. I already gave her all of the information, including a description of the young couple. I mentioned the purple camo backpack the guy was carrying. Dixie has a pretty good memory. She said she needed some time to dig through her records."

"Please let me know as soon as you hear anything," Carlita said.

"Will do." Reese gave her a thumbs up. "As soon as I hear back, I'll give you a buzz."

"Thanks for the lift." Carlita gave Reese a quick wave before following Mercedes inside. "She's a character."

"Yes, she is, and she definitely has connections. It's a shame we weren't able to glean any solid clues from the handbag," Mercedes said. "I wonder if or when we'll hear from the authorities again."

"Officer Clousen said it may take several days."

The door to Tony's former studio apartment opened. Vinnie stuck his head out. "I thought I heard voices."

"How was your shoe shopping adventure?" Mercedes teased.

"Let's just say I'm glad it's over. Brittney isn't feeling well. I think she ate something that didn't agree with her or the baby. She went to bed early, so it'll only be me for dinner."

Vinnie changed the subject. "There was a surprise visitor waiting on your back doorstep when we got here."

Chapter 18

"What kind of surprise visitor?"

"It was a cop. He said his name was Clousen something."

"Did he tell you what he wanted?"

"Nope. In fact, he didn't tell me he was a cop. He was dressed in street clothes, but I can pick them off a mile away."

"Great. I wonder if he tried calling." Carlita reached into her purse and pulled out her cell phone. "I don't have any messages."

"My guess is he wanted to catch you off guard," Vinnie said. "Cops are sneaky like that."

"I'm sure he'll be back. He probably wants to search the restaurant."

"Wouldn't he have asked to search it yesterday?" Mercedes asked.

"Who knows? All I know is I have nothing to hide and no crime has been committed." Carlita rubbed her brow. "I guess it's just the three of us for dinner since Paulie, Gina and the kids are going to hang out at the hotel tonight. Are you still planning on leaving in the morning?"

"Yeah. I gotta get back to work. Vito's guys are gettin' antsy to head out."

"Where are Vito's guys?" Carlita hadn't thought to ask where the two bodyguards might be staying.

"They're sleepin' in their car."

"You're kidding? How awful."

"Nah. They're used to it."

"I suppose." Carlita shifted her purse to her other hand. "Do you mind leftovers from the wedding?"

"Leftovers are fine. I'll follow you up." Vinnie quietly closed the door, checking to make sure it

221

was locked and then followed his mother up the stairs. Mercedes went on ahead and was already inside the apartment.

Vinnie chatted with his sister while Carlita warmed the food, careful not to touch the appetizers still boxed and in the back of the fridge.

After the food warmed, they filled their plates and carried them to the dining room table.

Carlita enjoyed the relaxed and quiet dinner with her two children. They discussed Vinnie's managerial job at the casino, the remodeled apartment in Atlantic City and the baby. They also talked about Ravello's Ristorante and the pawnshop. Finally, the topic turned to Megan Burelli.

"You find out for sure what happened to her?" Vinnie stabbed a meatball with his fork and took a big bite.

"Not yet. We're still leaning towards food poisoning, at least that's what Elvira said. If, and this is a big 'if' it was my food, it must have been one of the drinks or appetizers. She collapsed during the cocktail hour."

Carlita twirled spaghetti around her fork. "There were a coupla employees who took off before the reception ended. Pirate Pete spotted them out back, and then the trolley driver told Reese he picked up a couple matching Pete's description, at the trolley stop out front."

"They were acting strange," Mercedes added.

"Find out who they are and ask them to come in to talk to you."

"First, we have to figure out who they are. We think we may have gotten at least one of them on the video I recorded in the courtyard when we were waiting for the ambulance." Mercedes sprang from her chair and grabbed her cell phone off the desk.

She fiddled with the screen before handing it to her brother. "One of these may have been one of them, posing as an employee."

Vinnie squinted his eyes. "It's hard to tell anything from this tiny screen."

"I got a copy." Carlita grabbed her purse off the counter. She pulled out the printed copy of the two servers and handed it to her son.

"I recognize both of 'em. They were working the courtyard." He pointed at one of the women. "This one. She was serving the food. The second time she came around, I was gonna grab something, but she took off with the goods."

"With a tray full of food?" Carlita shook her head, confused.

"Yeah. That was definitely her." Vinnie started talking about something else, and Carlita only half-listened as she mulled over Vinnie's words. *Why would the woman leave with a tray full of food?*

Could it be the hit was only on Brittney? Was she the same woman Pete spotted, the one who was crying in the alley?

Maybe she was a remorseful killer, realizing she'd injured Megan Burelli, whom she believed was Brittney, and then decided she couldn't carry through in taking anyone else out.

Another troubling thought surfaced. If it were a paid hit, the woman's life would be in danger...her life and anyone else involved.

Carlita and her children discussed at length, the theory of Louie's soldiers infiltrating Ravello's restaurant staff with the sole purpose of taking Brittney...and possibly Vinnie, out by poisoning their food.

"Except they somehow got Megan Burelli and Brittney mixed up," Vinnie said. "They could easily have taken both of us out."

"With his bodyguards standing by watching, no less."

"The fact there are a couple of employees whose numbers have been disconnected is a clue," Mercedes said.

"I agree." Carlita polished off her last bite of leftover pizza. "Dominic might also be able to help. He was around them more than we were."

Vinnie finished his food and then glanced at his watch. "I better head back downstairs to check on Brittney."

Carlita reluctantly followed him to the door. "Your visit went by way too fast, Son."

"New Jersey ain't that far away, Ma. Why don't you and Mercedes come visit as soon as you get everything settled with the restaurant?"

"*If* we open our doors." A troubled look crossed Carlita's face. "If the authorities determine my food poisoned Megan Burelli, I might not have a restaurant to open."

"You'll be fine, Ma. If not, I'll come back down here and knock a few heads together."

"That should do the trick." Carlita watched her son make his way down the stairs before returning to the apartment. "I wonder if Tony and Shelby are ready to come home."

"Speaking of Tony and Shelby...how is Violet?" Mercedes asked.

"Oh my gosh. I forgot to check on Violet." Carlita fumbled inside her purse for her cell phone. "I promised Violet I would stop by to check on her. It completely slipped my mind." She dialed Paulie's cell phone. The call went to voice mail, so she tried Gina's number.

Thankfully, her daughter-in-law picked up. "Gina. It's me, Carlita. I promised Violet I would stop by to check on her. I forgot until now."

"She's on the sofa watching cartoons with the kids. Would you like to talk to her?"

"Yes, please."

Violet's small voice came on the line. "Hello?"

"Violet, this is Nana. How are you doing?"

"I'm good. I'm eating popcorn. We're watching Nemo."

"Are you having fun?"

"Uh-huh. We made a tent, and we're going to sleep in it tonight."

"So you want to spend the night with Aunt Gina and Uncle Paulie?"

"Yep. When is Mommy coming home?"

"She'll be home tomorrow."

"Okay." There was a muffled sound. "Bye, Nana."

"Bye, Violet." She was already gone. Gina returned to the line. "The kids are having fun."

"Thanks for watching Violet," Carlita said.

"You're welcome. Violet is keeping the others from fighting. She'll be a great big sister."

"Yes, I think you're right. She's a sweet little girl."

Gina promised to give her a call in the morning to let her know when they would be by to drop Violet off.

Carlita had a sudden thought. "Why don't you and Paulie have dinner or a night out before you leave? Mercedes and I would love to take the kids...not that we wouldn't love to spend time with you and Paulie, too."

Gina laughed. "I know what you mean. It would be nice. Sure."

"Great. It's a plan. Let me know what works for you." Carlita thanked Gina again for watching Violet and hung up the phone. "Violet is having a ball."

"See? You worried over nothing."

"I have to worry about something, don't I?" Carlita rubbed her eyes. "I think I'm going to head to bed. Tomorrow is shaping up to be a very long day."

She had no idea how accurate her statement would turn out to be.

Chapter 19

Carlita struggled to sleep. Every time she woke, she began worrying about something else.

First, was Megan Burelli's collapse. If the investigators determined Megan became ill after eating one of the wedding appetizers, what would stop the local authorities or the Georgia Department of Public Health, the department in charge of restaurant inspections, from shutting Ravello's down before it ever opened up?

Next on her list of worries was Violet's sleepover. She'd seemed excited when Carlita talked to her, that the children were "camping out."

If all of that wasn't enough, she wondered what possessed Elvira to buy the building across the alley. Perhaps her motivation was money. Not long ago, she'd snuck into the upper level of her apartment building and found an antique dagger hidden in one of the boxes.

Could it be Elvira unearthed more valuables upstairs and decided to buy the building, lock stock and barrel? Carlita wouldn't put anything past her former tenant if it involved money.

The thought of Elvira owning the building a stone's throw away was cause for concern. Her nosy neighbor would have no qualms about spying on her and her family. It was enough to make Carlita want to install surveillance cameras of her own.

Which brought up something else... she still needed to ask Elvira if she'd caught anything on her camera, a glimpse of whoever left the mysterious, unmarked box containing the headless cake topper on their doorstep.

Rambo was Carlita's regular alarm clock, but he was nowhere in sight when she woke the next morning. Bright sunlight beamed in through a crack in her bedroom curtains.

She slipped her robe on and then wandered into the living room. Mercedes was at the office desk, her hair pulled back in a ponytail, clad in a pair of sweatpants and a V-neck t-shirt.

"You're up early."

"Nana." Violet rolled off the sofa and hurtled her small body at Carlita.

"Violet." Carlita scooped her up. "How did you get here?"

"Gina called first thing this morning," Mercedes said. "Violet woke up sad and wanted to come home. I guess your cell phone was plugged into the charger in the kitchen, so she tried my number. You looked tired last night, so I wanted to let you sleep in. I took the trolley across town and picked Violet up."

Violet placed a chubby hand on each side of Carlita's cheek. "I woked up because I missed Rambo and Grayvie."

"I'm sure they missed you too." Carlita held her close. "And guess what else?"

"What?" Violet wiggled out of Carlita's arms.

"Mommy and Tony will be home today."

"Today." Violet hopped up and down. "I made them a special card. It's in my backpack."

"Are you hungry?" Carlita followed Violet into the kitchen.

"Aunt Mercedes bought me breakfast."

"We were hungry, so we grabbed some food at Colby's on our way home. I left a breakfast sandwich in the fridge for you," Mercedes said.

"What time is it?" Carlita glanced at the clock on the stove. "Oh my gosh. I thought I was up early. It's almost ten."

"We tried to keep quiet to let you sleep."

"Thanks, Mercedes."

"I already checked on Josh in the pawnshop. I also returned a couple of phone calls, on prospective tenants. One of them is interested in Shelby's unit. I told them they would have to wait a couple of days until Shelby finished moving out, to take a look at it."

"Perfect. We need to get those units rented as soon as possible." Carlita poured a cup of coffee and carried it into the dining room. "In case the health department shuts Ravello's down before it even opens."

"It won't happen," Mercedes said. "We still need to question the employees who were working Saturday."

"I agree. First, I want to stop by Pete's restaurant to see if he recognizes either of the women in the photo."

"Right. Why don't you grab a bite to eat and then get ready? We can go together."

Carlita wolfed down the breakfast sandwich and then headed to the bathroom. Mercedes and Violet were both ready and waiting for her when she finally emerged. "I want to stop by Elvira's place first, to see if her surveillance camera recorded whoever dropped the box with the headless you-know-what on the back step."

"I forgot about that," Mercedes said. "You have a sharper memory than I do, Ma."

"That's because I spent half the night, lying awake in bed worrying about everything. It's a wonder I got any sleep at all."

The trio crossed the alley, and Carlita knocked on Elvira's back door. The door opened a crack. She caught a glimpse of Dernice, peering out. "Yeah?"

"Is Elvira here?"

"She's taking care of an important business matter. She should be home soon."

"Maybe you can help." Carlita briefly explained wanting to check Elvira's video from Friday morning, the timeframe of when the headless cake topper was dropped off.

She didn't mention that Elvira hadn't technically *offered* to let Carlita see the video, and instead planned to use it as some sort of bargaining chip, yet to be determined.

Dernice lifted a brow. "She said you could see it?"

"I don't think those were her exact words. I believe she was going to let me have a look."

"Well...I suppose." The door opened wider, and Dernice motioned them inside to an area that reminded Carlita of a mini command post, complete with blinking red and blue lights beaming from an array of electronics.

"Welcome to EC Command Center." Dernice plopped down on the chair and reached for the mouse. "Let me see...the wedding was Saturday. You said the box in question arrived Friday morning?"

"Yes, Friday morning," Carlita confirmed.

"This surveillance equipment is slick. It's able to pick up any motion, and depending on your desired settings, it stores the images. Ours is set up to keep all images until we erase them. Elvira uses the video as her evening entertainment. You guys get some interesting guests coming and going, especially for Tony's wedding."

"You're spying on us all of the time?" Mercedes gasped.

"I wouldn't call it spying. Although Elvira does kind of have a thing for your hot new tenant, Sam Ivey. He doesn't appear to have a girlfriend. At least we haven't seen him with a woman." Dernice let out a low wolf whistle. "I have to admit he's a real looker."

"You can have him," Mercedes muttered. "He's a jerk."

"Really?" Mercedes' glaring dislike for Sam got Dernice's attention. "He seems like a real gentleman. He helped me bring my motorcycle inside the other day when it started to rain."

"Mercedes and he got off on the wrong foot, and now she doesn't like him."

"Plus, he's spying on us," Mercedes said. "Everyone is spying on us."

"Hold up. Looks like we got something." Dernice clicked on the screen to enlarge the picture. "It appears someone dropped a package off on your back stoop around seven forty-five. Check it out."

Carlita leaned in to study the image. "Mercedes...do you see what I see?"

"Yep. It's a male wearing a purple camo backpack."

"Let's see what else we got." Dernice tapped the keyboard and they watched as the man dropped a brown box on the step. He looked around before jogging in the direction of the restaurant, and out of sight.

"That's him. A hundred bucks says this is the guy Pirate Pete spotted in the alley during the wedding, with a young woman who was obviously distressed.

He's the one who left the headless cake topper." Carlita studied the image. "I'm beginning to think this young man was working in my kitchen during the wedding."

Mercedes tapped Dernice's shoulder. "Is there a way to forward this image to us by text or in an email?"

"Of course. It's fairly simple," Dernice said. "You think this guy may have been involved in the food poisoning incident in the courtyard?"

"Yes. I believe that he, along with a young woman he was with, poisoned one of the wedding guests, but why?" Carlita thought about Brittney and Vinnie. Were they the targets? If they were, why hadn't the woman followed through and poisoned Vinnie at the same time as Megan Burelli, who Carlita now suspected was mistaken for Brittney?

"I need a copy of this image to see if Pirate Pete can positively identify him. I've already got the print of the female courtyard server."

"I don't know if I can," Dernice said. "Not until I discuss it with Elvira. She's not one to hand out freebies without getting something in return."

"Good grief." Carlita rolled her eyes. "Birds of a feather. Name your price."

The back door creaked open, and Elvira stepped inside. "Hello."

"Hello, Elvira." Carlita motioned to the shovel she was carrying. "Have you been out digging ditches?"

"Not quite." She eyed Carlita and Mercedes suspiciously. "What are you doing here?"

"We took a look at your surveillance video from the other morning, to see if it caught the person who left the box with the headless cake topper inside on camera. It did, and we were bargaining with Dernice to obtain a copy of the image."

"What kind of bargain?" Elvira propped the shovel in the corner. "It better be good."

"What do you want?"

"Well, I have been giving it some thought. I was thinking along the lines of a dinner invite at your place, along with your hot new tenant, Sam Ivey."

"I told you she was gaga over Sam," Dernice said.

"I thought you were in love with Cool Bones," Mercedes said.

"Unfortunately, our personalities just don't mesh."

"Imagine that," Carlita snorted. "Tell you what...I'll work on it. You have my word. I need the image before I can arrange the dinner date. Please send it to Mercedes' phone."

"Are you willing to put our deal in writing?"

"I already promised, and you have witnesses."

Elvira pursed her lips thoughtfully. "Okay. Fair warning...I'm going to hound you until it happens."

"Threatening won't help."

"No, it's a promise." Elvira nodded to her sister. "Go ahead and send it to Mercedes' cell phone."

"It's done." Dernice shifted to face her sister. "How did the closing go?"

"Your closing was today?" Carlita glanced at her cell phone. "I got the text."

"Yep. This property is all mine now," Elvira beamed. "I bought it lock, stock and barrel. The first thing I'm going to do is tear down the wall, so we can go up and down the stairs instead of having to crawl up the fire escape."

"That's why you bought this place, isn't it?" Carlita asked. "Because you think there are more valuable items upstairs."

"Maybe. I did Davis a favor. He was happy to leave the junk upstairs behind. He inherited it when he bought the building years ago. It's mine now, and I intend to sort through my newly-acquired belongings with a fine tooth comb."

"Tearing this place apart oughta keep you out of trouble for a few days," Mercedes joked.

Carlita's cell phone vibrated. "Uh-oh. Reese sent me a text. She wants me to call her back right away." She thanked Elvira again for emailing the image and ushered Violet out of the building.

They waited for Mercedes to close the door behind them before Carlita dialed Reese's cell phone. "You found something out from Dixie over at the bus station."

"Yes. I have a positive ID on the man and woman. She confirmed the man was wearing a purple camo backpack and they fit the description. They each purchased an e-ticket headed for Miami, Florida, but they never boarded the bus."

"So they're still in the area?"

"You could say that. At least one of them is still in the area. You haven't watched the morning news I take it."

"No. Why?"

"The authorities haven't publicly released the name yet, but they found one of them dead behind the bus station late last night."

Chapter 20

It took a minute for Reese's statement to sink in. "Dead?"

"Yes. It was the woman. Dixie told me her name is Monica Clay, and she was murdered. Does the name ring a bell?"

"Monica Clay," Carlita whispered to Mercedes. "Is that the name of one of our restaurant workers?"

"It sounds kinda familiar."

"We'll have to check," Carlita told Reese. "What about the guy with the purple backpack?"

"I have his information along with the dead girl's. From what Dixie was able to glean during the police questioning, he's MIA."

Reese continued. "Could be he and the woman argued, he killed her and then knowing the bus station had his contact information, not to mention they could track his ticket, he took off."

"True. What a mess," Carlita said.

"I've got it all. Names, addresses, cell phone numbers. Dixie sent it to me before the cops showed up. I gotta get going. The trolley is almost loaded here at the main depot. I'll send it to you in between stops."

"Thanks, Reese. You're the best."

Carlita ended the call and slipped the phone into her pocket. "Let's head over to talk to Pete. I think we may be onto something. Reese has the names of the guy with the purple camo backpack and his companion, their cell phone numbers and addresses."

"Awesome. We can match them to what we have on file for the restaurant employees."

"If Pete can confirm the identity of the female server in the video, along with the picture Elvira's surveillance camera picked up of the man dropping off the mysterious cake topper, we're onto something."

"I'm hungry," Violet said.

"We'll run by Pirate Pete's place and then when we come back, I'll make you a peanut butter and jelly sandwich," Carlita promised.

"Okay. Can I have some cookies?"

"Yes, if you wait until we get home, you can have Italian cookies, too."

Mercedes led Violet and her mother off to the side. "I think we should send the video of the woman in the courtyard and Elvira's surveillance camera shot of the man to Reese. We'll ask her to forward both to Dixie to see if she can positively identify them, as well."

"Great idea. Text Pete and let him know we're on the way, too." Carlita waited for Mercedes to send the pictures and a text to Reese and Pirate Pete before the trio began walking again. "I hope Pete is at the Pirate House."

"If not, he's at the dock and The Flying Gunner. It's an easy walk either way."

"I want to see the pirates again," Violet chimed in.

"Wherever we end up, I hope it's indoors." The summer sun beat down on them as they walked, and Carlita's shirt grew damp as her armpits began to perspire. She wasn't sure if it was the heat or the fact they might actually be one step closer to figuring out what happened to Megan Burelli.

If it was a case of Louie's henchman trying to take Vinnie and Brittney out and they hadn't succeeded, her son and daughter-in-law were still in imminent danger. They needed to start piecing the puzzle together and fast!

The restaurant wasn't open yet. Carlita knocked lightly on the entrance door.

A man appeared in the doorway. "We don't open for another hour."

"I know. I'm here to see Pete if he's in."

"Your name?"

"Carlita Garlucci."

The door abruptly slammed in her face and Carlita jumped back. "Whoa."

"How rude," Mercedes fumed. "He didn't even tell us if Pete was here or to wait a minute."

"If he doesn't come back in a couple of minutes, we'll try The Flying Gunner."

The door swung open, and Pirate Pete joined them on the porch. "I got yer text. I was gettin' ready to answer when Joey told me you were here. Come in." He motioned them inside. "Any news on your wedding guest's condition?"

"No." Carlita patted Violet's head. "Is there somewhere we can talk? Little ears..."

"Ah." Pirate Pete held up a finger. "Let me see if Susie is around. She can accompany Violet to the kitchen for a cookie."

"I love cookies."

Pete disappeared behind a swinging door and returned with a young woman. "This is Susie. She's going to let you pick out a cookie and then bring you to my office."

"Okay." Violet took the young woman's hand and they headed toward the kitchen.

"So there's nothing new on the wedding guest," Pete prompted.

"No, but we now have a dead woman possibly linked to my restaurant," Carlita said. "We think the woman you saw crying in the alley the other day was found dead out behind the bus station."

"You're kidding!"

"I wish I was."

Pete waited until they were inside his office before closing the door behind them. "What happened?"

Carlita briefly recapped everything she knew; starting with the two workers she suspected had been hired to murder Vinnie and Brittney. She mentioned the trolley, the bus station, Elvira's surveillance footage of the mysterious man and ended with the body. "If you can positively identify the man who left the headless cake topper and the female server in the courtyard, we may have our suspects."

Carlita handed Pete the photocopy of the female servers Mercedes had printed off. "Do you recognize either of these women?"

Pete slipped his reading glasses on and studied the picture. "Aye. That be her, the one on the right, except she wasn't wearing a uniform when I saw her." He handed the photocopy back. "You say you have a picture of the man, too?"

"Yes. Elvira's surveillance camera caught him dropping off the unmarked box on my back step."

Mercedes tapped her cell phone screen and passed it to Pete. "This is the man."

Carlita watched as Pete studied the picture. "That be him. See the black server uniform he's wearing?"

"No." Carlita hurried behind the desk and peered over Pete's shoulder. "You're right. I never noticed the uniform. So, you're saying these two *were* the ones you spotted in the alley, and the woman was crying."

"Yes."

"If Dixie at the bus station can confirm these are the same two, and we can match their contact information to what we have on the job applications, I think we have Megan Burelli's poisoner."

"But who killed the woman, Monica Clay?" Mercedes asked.

"My gut tells me it was the young man who was with her," Carlita theorized. "It makes the most sense."

"Have you heard from the newlyweds?" Pete asked.

"Yes. Shelby called to check on Violet a couple of times. They're coming home today."

There was a muffled tap at the door. It creaked open, and Susie escorted Violet inside.

"Did you eat your cookie already?" Carlita asked.

"She ate two," Susie laughed. "I stopped her from eating a third."

"Thank you, Susie," Pete said.

"No problem." Susie pulled the door shut behind her.

Carlita clutched Violet's sticky hand. "We're going to nickname you the cookie monster."

"Mommy is bringing me a special surprise."

"I bet she's bringing you a shark," Pete teased.

"I don't want a shark."

"I'm sure it's not a shark," Carlita said. "We better get going." She turned to Pete. "Thank you for meeting with us. You've been very helpful."

"Don't forget about our Savannah restaurant group's meeting on Wednesday. It's at Russo's restaurant this time." Pete led them out of his office, through the restaurant and to the parking lot. "He's expanding his operations and adding catering facilities."

"That's a good idea," Carlita said. "I'll be curious to see how that works out. It's something we may look at down the road."

"I thought about gettin' into it myself a few years back, but then I bought me a pirate ship."

"You stay busy enough. I guess I'll see you on Wednesday. I plan to tell the authorities what we've found so far, right after I'm able to confirm Monica and the missing man were employed by me."

Carlita thanked Pete again for meeting them on such short notice, and joined Mercedes and Violet in the parking lot.

The walk home was at a brisk pace, thanks to Violet, who pulled them along.

They turned the corner and came to an abrupt halt when a strange vehicle blocked their path.

Chapter 21

The vehicle was unfamiliar, but the man standing on the stoop was easily recognizable. "Officer Clousen."

"Hello, Mrs. Garlucci. I left a message earlier asking if I could swing by. When you didn't reply, I figured I would take my chances."

"I...didn't get a message." Carlita glanced at her cell phone. "Oh wait. I see a missed call."

"I wanted to let you know Ms. Burelli passed away early this morning. It may be some time before we get an official word on the cause of death. In the meantime, I have a few questions."

Carlita motioned to Mercedes. "You better take Violet inside."

"This should only take a minute."

Mercedes ushered the small girl inside the building, and the police officer waited until the door closed behind them.

"Are you aware of any of your other wedding guests becoming ill during the wedding reception?"

"No, not that I know of," Carlita answered honestly. "As far as I know, Ms. Burelli was the only one."

"Your wait staff...were they regular employees or hired by a third party to serve the guests?"

"They were hired employees, but new hires. My restaurant will be opening for the first time later this week. I've never worked with the employees before Saturday's wedding."

"And you screened them before hiring, as in background checks, that sort of thing," Clousen said.

"Yes, of course. The same way we do when we hire our pawnshop employees and the same way we screen our tenants before signing a lease."

"That's what I thought. I appreciate your time, Mrs. Garlucci. I'll be sure to let you know as soon as I hear anything else."

"You're welcome. I...I feel terrible," Carlita said.

"I can see you do," Clousen said kindly. "Thanks again for your time."

"Before you go." Carlita motioned to the officer. "We have had a couple of strange incidents occur, right before my son's wedding and Ms. Burelli's collapse."

Carlita briefly told him about the mysterious cake topper and the break-in at the restaurant.

The officer jotted down a few notes. He paused when she got to the part about the break-in. "What did the intruders take?"

"Nothing," Carlita said.

"Nothing?" The officer paused, pen midair. "Nothing at all?"

"Not that I'm aware of, which is odd," Carlita said.

He flipped the cover of the notepad and shoved it in his pocket. "You could file a police report, for insurance purposes, but the fact that nothing was stolen..."

"I know."

She felt foolish for mentioning the cake topper. The officer probably believed it had been shipped to their home by mistake. "I'll let you know if I think of anything else."

"I'll be in touch." The officer climbed into his unmarked patrol car and backed out of the alley.

Carlita slowly made her way inside and trudged up the stairs. She could hear excited chatter coming from within and a male voice. She swung the door open and found Shelby and Tony seated on the sofa. Violet was sandwiched between them.

"Mommy's home!" Violet exclaimed.

"They sure are." Carlita hugged her son and daughter-in-law. "You both look rested."

"The honeymoon was wonderful." Tony reached for his bride's hand. "Thank you so much for watching Violet, for giving us a wonderful wedding, Ma."

"You're welcome. We missed you, but are glad you were able to enjoy a couple of days off."

"I talked to Paulie. We're gonna meet him and Gina for dinner. You're welcome to join us," Tony said.

"Maybe. I have some other things to take care of. I'll let you know later," Carlita said. "Mercedes might want to tag along."

Mercedes, who was sitting nearby, nodded. "I might."

"We brought you something." Shelby handed Carlita a gift bag.

"What is this?" Carlita opened the bag and peered inside. She gently lifted out an antique wooden box.

"It's an Italian music box," Shelby said. "The shopkeeper told us it was a one of a kind, handcrafted Sorrento, and carved from precious, rare woods."

Carlita ran a light hand over the top before carefully lifting the lid. It began to play O' Sole Mio. She briefly closed her eyes and hummed along. "It's beautiful. I love it."

"Shelby picked it out. She found it in a gift shop," Tony said.

"How thoughtful, both of you. Thank you."

"You're welcome." Shelby covered her mouth as a yawn escaped. "Excuse me. Riding in the car made me sleepy."

"We should get going. We have some unpacking to do and laundry to take care of. I wanna stop by the pawnshop and check on things." Tony stood.

"I don't blame you. I'm sure Violet is ready to go home."

Shelby rubbed her daughter's back. "Were you a good girl for Nana?"

"Yes. We rode on the pirate ship and squirted squirt guns, and then we hunted for treasure. I got to swim in the hotel pool and slept in a fort."

"My goodness. It sounds like you had a wonderful time while we were gone. Give Nana a hug good-bye and tell her thank you."

Carlita hugged Violet. "Thank *you* for keeping Mercedes and me company."

"And Rambo and Grayvie," Violet hugged her back. "Can I take a cookie with me?"

"Of course." Carlita quickly packaged a few of her homemade cookies and handed them to Violet. "Be a good girl for Mommy and Tony."

Violet promised she would before hopping down the steps to wait for her mother and stepfather.

Carlita closed the door behind them and leaned against it. "Is it me or has it been a very long few days?"

"They've been pretty long. While you were catching up with Tony and Shelby, I checked your email. Reese sent over the information from Dixie. I thought you might want to see if there's a match between the restaurant employees and the couple who bought the bus tickets."

"I do." Carlita made a beeline for the computer. She sat at the desk while Mercedes pulled up a chair. "I already sorted through the files. This shouldn't take long."

Carlita found Reese's email and highlighted the first name...Blake Tanner. "This name doesn't sound familiar."

Mercedes thumbed through the applications. "I don't see anyone by the name of Blake Tanner. Let me double check." She flipped through the sheets again. "Nope. No such name. Let's try to match him to an address or cell phone number."

"Try One Fifteen Hamilton Street."

"Hamilton...Hamilton. I see a One Fifteen Hamilton Street. It's the address for Duane Sorensen. His was one of the disconnected cell phone numbers." Mercedes waved the application in the air. "We got a winner. I think Duane Sorensen is Blake Tanner or vice versa."

"Great. Now let's see what we have for Monica Clay," Carlita said.

Mercedes grew quiet as she sorted through the stack again. "Bingo. Monica Clay. Guess what address she listed?"

"One Fifteen Hamilton Street."

"Yes. We have a connection. We have names. We have addresses..."

"And we have a disconnected cell phone," Carlita said. "What number did Ms. Clay list as a contact number?"

"Now that I take a closer look, she used the same disconnected number Duane, aka Blake, used. At least we have a physical address."

"Blake and Monica listed the same address and were both hired by Dominic and approved by me. I think it's time to have a chat with Dominic. Maybe he noticed something the other day at the wedding reception."

"Should we tell the authorities?" Mercedes asked.

"I'm sure they're already investigating Ms. Clay's death and looking for Duane or Blake, or whoever he is. We can fill Officer Clousen in on the connection." Carlita reached for her cell phone. "I'm going to call him right now."

The officer didn't answer, so she left a message, telling him she had some interesting information she wanted to share. "It's only a matter of time before the authorities show up on our doorstep, asking about Ms. Clay's employment, as well as Blake Tanner or Duane Sorensen."

Carlita drummed her fingers on the desk. "I wonder how long it will take for Reese to show Dixie the photos and video, to see if she recognizes Monica or Blake or Duane."

Chirp. Carlita's cell phone rang, startling her and she jumped. "It's Vinnie." She pressed the answer button. "Hello, Son. You must have read my mind. I was going to call you."

"I just wanted to let you know that we made it home safe and sound. What's up?"

"Let me put you on speaker, so Mercedes can hear." Carlita pressed the speaker button. "Officer Clousen stopped by. Megan Burelli died this morning."

There was a long pause on the other end. "You're kidding."

"No. Vito's guys, have they headed back to New York yet?"

"Yeah. We parted ways in Jersey. Why?"

"Because the woman who tried to serve you food and then abruptly took it away...the same one who served Megan Burelli the appetizers right before she collapsed, is dead. Her body was found behind the bus station early this morning."

Vinnie cleared his throat. "Are you sure?"

"Almost a hundred percent. I think she and her accomplice were plants, sent to poison you and Brittney. Instead, they poisoned the wrong person. When they realized what had happened, they panicked and took off."

"They took off for the bus station?" Vinnie asked. "Why not go into hiding until the heat is off?"

"How you gonna hide from the family?" Carlita asked. "They bought a coupla bus tickets. Before they could get out, Monica, the female server, was murdered. The man, Blake or Duane, we're still not sure which is his real name, he took off, and we think he's on the run. He could be dead, too, and his body hasn't turned up yet."

"Unless this Blake or Duane, the accomplice, killed her and took off," Vinnie said.

"It could be," Carlita admitted. "But I'm leaning more toward it being Louie's henchman. It was a botched assassination attempt with you and Brittney as the targets. When it didn't work, the plants realized they needed to get out of town before Louie found out."

Mercedes chimed in. "Vito wouldn't send his guys all the way to Savannah if he didn't think there was a credible threat."

"True. I'm gonna give Vito a call, see what he knows. I'll get back with you."

"In the meantime, be careful," Carlita said. "If Louie finds out you're still alive, he might try again."

"There's plenty of security here at the casino. It's like Fort Knox, but we'll be careful."

"That makes me feel a little better." She told her son she loved him and then disconnected the line.

"I'm getting a bad feeling. Something isn't sitting right."

The doorbell rang. "I bet Paulie and Gina are stopping by." Carlita hurried down the steps and to the back door. She swung it open and found a solemn faced Officer Clousen.

There was another man with him, Carlita recognized from previous investigations handled by the local law enforcement. It was Detective Polivich.

"Hello, Officer Clousen, Detective Polivich. You got my message?"

"Yes. I got your message. We also received an anonymous tip from our crime hotline. The caller claimed to be an employee of yours. He stated you intentionally poisoned Ms. Burelli before killing one of your restaurant employees and dumping her body behind the bus station."

Chapter 22

"We'd like for you to accompany us to the police station for more questioning."

Carlita stared at the officer in disbelief. "That's crazy. What possible reason would I have for poisoning one of the guests at my son's wedding?"

Mercedes, hearing the commotion downstairs, joined her mother. "What's going on?"

"An anonymous tipster called the local crime hotline, claiming I poisoned Megan Burelli. I then killed one of my restaurant employees and dumped her body behind the bus station. They want me to go to the police station with them to answer some questions."

"They think you killed Monica Clay?"

Detective Polivich lifted a brow. "You know the deceased woman's name? Her name hasn't yet been released."

"I...uh. We have a friend who works at the bus station. She told us," Mercedes sputtered. "Besides, we weren't hiding anything. In fact, we tried calling you."

"Maybe you both should come in for questioning," Polivich replied.

Faced with the seriousness of the situation, the warning bells went off in Carlita's head. Megan Burelli - poisoned at her son's wedding. Monica Clay, an employee, murdered and her body dumped behind the bus station. "Before we do that, I think we need to have an attorney present."

"We can't force you to go with us." Polivich switched strategies. "What information did you have for Officer Clousen?"

"We were actually going to show him video footage. We believe Duane Sorensen, who also goes by the name of Blake Tanner, we're not sure which is his real name, was with Ms. Clay. We think Monica Clay served Megan Burelli poisoned food or drink," Carlita said.

"Tanner aka Sorensen, also purchased a bus ticket. He was a new employee of ours, and if my theory is correct, he was one of the last people to see Monica Clay alive," Mercedes said. "Why don't you question him?"

"We will as soon as we find him," Polivich said. "Where's the video footage?"

"On my phone." Mercedes whipped her cell phone out of her back pocket. She pulled up Elvira's surveillance camera recording and handed the phone to the detective. "This man, we now believe is Duane Sorensen or Blake Tanner, also an employee of Ravello's, left an unmarked box on our back step right where we're standing, either to scare us or as a threat. We're not sure of the reason."

Detective Polivich viewed the brief footage before passing the phone to Officer Clousen. "What was in the box?"

"It was a wedding cake topper, and the groom's head was missing. One of the wedding guests, Pirate Pete Taylor, spotted Sorensen/Taylor and Monica Clay in this alley, near the dumpster during the wedding reception. The woman appeared visibly upset, and according to Pete, she was crying."

Carlita briefly told them they were able to trace the couple's steps, how they rode the trolley across town and got off at the bus station. "The regular trolley route driver, also a family friend, is Claryce Magillicuddy. She didn't witness the couple boarding the trolley. Her fill-in, Jim someone, did."

"What if the anonymous caller was Blake Tanner? What if he murdered Monica Clay and is trying to make it look like we killed her, along with Megan Burelli?" Mercedes asked.

Polivich and Clousen exchanged a quick look, and Carlita suspected they were already investigating that angle. "Tell you what, we'll contact our attorney and get back with you on when we'll be available to come down for questioning. In the meantime, I would take a closer look at Duane Sorensen/Blake Tanner instead of harassing an innocent business owner."

"We're only doing our job," the detective said. "You were named specifically, and it's our job to follow up on every lead."

"And I'm sure you're investigating Megan Burelli's death as suspicious," Carlita said.

"Yes."

Mercedes took her phone from the officer. "I'm going to throw this theory out there. It could be our new employee, Monica Clay, a restaurant server, intentionally poisoned Megan Burelli. Megan was a target along with other multiple potential targets, she panicked or changed her mind and didn't follow through, which is why Pete found her and her accomplice out back and she was visibly upset."

Carlita picked up. "They left Walton Square via the trolley and got off at the bus station, where they purchased two tickets, planning to leave town. Maybe they argued. Maybe Tanner killed Monica Clay and is in hiding."

"You must have your own suspicions to suggest such a theory. Is there someone else, perhaps a guest or family member who may have been a target?" Clousen asked. "Perhaps someone from up north?"

Carlita's mouth went dry. Savannah was a small town and rumors ran rampant. She was well aware some acquaintances suspected she and her family moved to Savannah to escape their past...surely, the authorities would know that, too.

"Two of your sons still live up north," Polivich said quietly. "I don't know if I ever recall hearing what your sons do for a living."

"Paulie, my youngest, is mayor of a small town," Carlita said. "But he's not a crooked politician; I can assure you of that."

"What about the other son?" Polivich prompted.

"He works for his father-in-law in New Jersey."

"At a casino," Clousen said. "We've done a little digging around before we drove over here. Let's not beat around the bush. Is there any reason to suspect a guest or worker at the wedding was targeting someone other than Ms. Burelli?"

Carlita and Mercedes exchanged an uneasy glance.

"Maybe. I mean, we don't have anything concrete," she blurted out. "I didn't poison Burelli. I didn't even know her, and barely knew Monica Clay. I just hired her."

"How well did you know Blake Tanner?" Clousen asked.

"His real name is Blake Tanner?"

"Yes."

"He gave us a fake name of Duane Sorensen." Carlita crossed her arms. "I'm not going to say anything else until I talk to my attorney."

"We'll be waiting for your call, Mrs. Garlucci." Detective Polivich handed her his card before he and the police officer climbed into their car and drove off.

"Great," Mercedes muttered. "They think we had something to do with Burelli and Clay's deaths. Who do you think called the crime hotline and named you as the killer?"

"Blake Tanner." Rambo nudged the back door open and joined Carlita and her daughter on the stoop. "It has to be Tanner. There's no way the family called a crime tip hotline to implicate us. They could care less who takes the fall. I think if the cops focus their attention on Tanner, they'll have the real killer."

"You gonna go down to the police station with a lawyer?" Mercedes asked.

"I dunno. I'm kinda hoping with the information we gave them, they'll forget about harassing us and track down the real culprit, Blake Tanner. First, we need to find a lawyer, one who specializes in criminal law, not real estate." Carlita sighed heavily. "I hope Vinnie took my advice and is on guard. I don't think this is the end. Maybe it's just the beginning."

"Makes you wonder what Vito did to Louie to make him go after Vito's family."

"I don't know." Carlita eyed Rambo. "I could use some fresh air to clear my head."

"I'll go with you. Let me grab Rambo's leash." Mercedes darted back inside, her feet clattering loudly on the stairs.

When she didn't return, Carlita stuck her head inside. She heard the sound of loud voices coming from the upstairs hall.

A flushed Mercedes appeared at the top of the stairs. She shot a sour look over her shoulder and tromped down the steps.

"What's going on?"

"Ivey's apartment door was open again, so I took the liberty of shutting it for him on my way out. He didn't like it."

"Mercedes," Carlita chided. "Does it bother you that much if Sam leaves his door ajar?"

"Yes, it bothers me that much. He's spying on us, and even if you don't care, I do."

"He's not spying." Carlita hooked Rambo's leash. They began walking toward the parking lot and Rambo's favorite strip of grass. "Have you ever stopped to think maybe he's lonely?"

"Well, then he should get a dog or a cat or a parrot."

Carlita wrinkled her nose. "I wish I could figure out why you dislike him so much."

"Because he's a pompous jerk, he's full of himself and he's nosy."

Carlita let the statement slide as they made their way into the parking lot. She followed behind her pooch as he inspected the grassy area.

Mercedes leaned against the car. "Watch out for Rambo's land mines."

"I need to get out here and clean up the parking lot and this grassy area. It's time to mow." Carlita waded through the deep grass, keeping an eye out for Rambo's poo piles.

She stepped into a hole and lost her balance, falling onto her hands and knees. "What in the world?"

Carlita lifted her foot and peered into a freshly dug hole. She said the first thing that came to mind. "Elvira!"

Chapter 23

"Are you all right?" Mercedes rushed forward to help her mother.

"I'm fine, but Elvira might not be after I get my hands on her. I'm going to wring her neck." Carlita scowled at the gaping hole. "Now I know what she was doing with a shovel."

"Why would Elvira dig a hole in our yard?"

"Remember the story Pete told us about some of these older Savannah area properties, and how it's not uncommon to find valuables hidden or even buried in the backyards?"

"Yeah," Mercedes nodded. "It was during the Civil War era. The city fell into ruin, and the majority of area treasures went missing when the property owners fled or abandoned their properties."

"I'm certain that's why Elvira was gung ho on buying her building. She found the antiques upstairs, and she's probably convinced there are even more valuables buried around here." Carlita brushed off her knees and glared at her former tenant's building.

"What are you going to do?"

Carlita lifted a finger. "Do you hear that?"

"Hear what?" Mercedes asked.

"Listen." A faint beeping noise echoed from the vicinity of the shrubs that separated her property from Elvira's property.

Carlita marched around the corner and nearly collided with Elvira, clad in denim capris and wearing a wide brimmed hat. She stood in the middle of her yard, holding a metal detector.

"What are you doing?"

She barely gave Carlita a glance. "Looking for buried treasure."

"Yeah, well you're digging up private property. There's a hole in my yard, right in front of my parking lot. I nearly broke my neck."

"My detector went off. I needed to check it out."

"That's my property."

"Don't get your panties in a bunch. I was going to fill it in."

Carlita spied a shovel propped up against the side of the building. "I want it filled in immediately, before one of my tenants or an animal gets hurt, and I get sued."

"I could see where it might create a hazard. Not that I blame you. You have enough problems." Elvira hummed as she hovered the detector over a patch of loose gravel. "How's your investigation going?"

"Someone placed an anonymous call to the police department's crime hotline. They told the authorities I not only murdered Megan Burelli, but also one of my servers."

"Burelli died? I didn't know that." Elvira turned the detector off, giving Carlita her full attention. "Did you tell the authorities we caught a man on camera leaving an unmarked box on your step?"

"Yes, and I was able to positively identify him as one of my new restaurant employees, Blake Tanner or Duane Sorensen, I'm not sure which is his real name."

"You need to do a better job of screening your employees," Elvira said. "You should consider using my company for background checks. EC Investigative Services has both the tools and experience to ensure you get topnotch workers, not thugs and criminals."

"Ugh." Carlita clenched her fists, her fingernails digging into the palm of her hands. "I did not hire thugs. In fact, my manager, who came highly recommended and vetted, screened each and every employee before hiring them."

"He didn't do such a hot job either." Elvira resumed her metal detecting. "How are you doing on hooking me up with your hottie new tenant, Sam?"

"I haven't worked on it yet. I've been a little busy. I'll talk to Sam later today or tomorrow if I'm not sitting in a jail cell."

"Don't be so dramatic."

"I'm not being dramatic." Carlita's voice lowered, and the urge to throttle Elvira was growing by the minute. "I have some serious problems. I have a dead wedding guest and a dead restaurant worker with a second employee on the run."

The metal detector beeped loudly. Elvira balanced the detector in one hand and reached for her shovel.

"Hold this." She thrust the detector in Mercedes' hand and began shoveling dirt.

Clink. "I hit something." Elvira dropped the shovel and dug with her hands.

"You're crazy."

"You won't think so when I find a mess of gold coins or something historic and valuable." Elvira dumped the dirt off to the side and continued digging. "I could be sitting on a gold mine...literally."

"I give up." Carlita threw her hands in the air. "Don't forget to fill in my hole and for the record, you do not have my permission to dig any more holes on my property."

"You'll be changing your tune as soon as I find something." Elvira stopped digging and peered into the sizable hole. "I see something shiny."

She reached into her back pocket and pulled out a trowel. "I knew there was something buried around here." Elvira dug in a circle, widening the hole.

She tossed the trowel off to the side, stuck her hand in the hole and pulled out a silver coin.

"Check it out. It's a silver coin." She handed it to Carlita.

"I'll be darned. You did find a coin."

"Of course I did."

Carlita and Mercedes watched as Elvira unearthed three more silver coins before eyeing them suspiciously. "This is my property. I don't want you messing around over here."

"Like you were messing around on my property?"

"We've already been over this. I'll fill in the hole." Elvira held out her hand. "Coin please."

Carlita handed it to her. "I'll get back with you as soon as I have a chance to talk to Sam." She, along with Mercedes and Rambo, started to walk away.

"Hey, Carlita."

Carlita paused.

"It sounds like Burelli's poisoning was an inside job. I would take a closer look at your employees."

"I'm meeting with my restaurant manager later this afternoon. Maybe he can shed some light on the restaurant employee found dead and the other one who is MIA."

"Yep." Elvira nodded. "Let me know if you need any help."

Carlita nodded toward the hole. "Good luck with your treasure hunt."

"Thanks."

Carlita and Mercedes tiptoed across the grassy strip, keeping an eye out for more holes. They circled the block and then slowly made their way back upstairs.

"I better grab a bite to eat before I head next door to meet Dominic."

"Elvira was right. Dominic might be able to give you a little more feedback on the employees," Mercedes said. "I wonder if the authorities will want to talk to him and the restaurant employees. I'm surprised they didn't ask to see our employee applications."

"My guess is they will after they're done with me." Carlita headed to the kitchen to warm up some leftover soup and fix a sandwich.

Rambo followed her, watching her every move.

"Beggar," she patted his head. "You can have one small slice of roast beef. Grayvie, too."

"I'm gonna head to my room," Mercedes said. "Before I forget, we got a couple of promising applications for tenants. I ditched a few I didn't think were good matches and emailed the others to you."

"Great. I'll look at them while I eat." Carlita fed each of her pets a treat before piling roast beef on a slice of bread. She smeared a thick layer of mayonnaise on a second slice before adding lettuce and tomato. She carried the soup and sandwich to her desk and settled in.

After a quick check of the bank accounts, she opened her email and found Mercedes' message and an attachment with the tenant applications.

She decided both looked promising and sent a reply to Mercedes, telling her both sounded like good fits, but the decision was ultimately up to her daughter.

Carlita polished off the homemade minestrone and roast beef on seeded rye before carrying her dirty dishes to the kitchen. There was just enough time to freshen up and head next door to meet Dominic.

"Hey, Mercedes." Carlita rapped lightly on her daughter's door and jumped back, waiting for it to fly open. She wasn't disappointed.

"Hey, Ma. I got your message. You want me to go ahead and meet with the potential tenants?"

"Yes. The ball is in your court now, Mercedes. I trust your judgment."

"Thanks." Mercedes grinned, the dimple in her cheek deepening. "You heading over to chat with Dominic?"

"Yes. I better get going, or I'm going to be late. You wanna go with me?"

"Nah. I want to get a little writing in and then head down to check on Tony."

"Which reminds me. I think we should join the others for dinner later. I figured we could head to Russo's restaurant. Now that I'm a member of the restaurant group, I think we should try to support each other's businesses."

She thanked her daughter for taking care of weeding through the prospective tenants and then wandered down the steps. Carlita passed the parking lot and caught a glimpse of Elvira, still digging holes on her property.

She stepped inside the restaurant and discovered Dominic had already arrived and was rifling through the filing cabinet.

"Hey, Dominic."

"Hello, Carlita. What happened to the employee applications that were in the filing cabinet?"

"I took them out the other day. They're in my home office."

"I...need the applications." Dominic shut the cabinet door. "Two of the new workers quit on Saturday, during the wedding reception."

"That's the first I've heard of anyone quitting." Carlita wondered if Dominic was talking about Monica Clay and the person she knew as Duane Sorensen/Blake Tanner.

"What with the guest keeling over, I figured you had your hands full, and I didn't want to add to your troubles. I was thinking I could take a second look at the applicants we didn't hire."

"I'll bring the folders back over later."

"I need them now."

Carlita lifted a brow, taken aback by the tone of his voice. "I'll bring them over later," she repeated. "If you recall, we hired a few extra workers in case someone quit."

"That was our original plan. I'm having second thoughts. I think we're stretching our staff too thin."

The warning bells went off in Carlita's head. Dominic knew about Monica Clay's death.

"You heard the body of one of the servers, Monica Clay, was found out behind the bus station," Carlita said quietly. "Is she one of the workers who quit?" The pieces were beginning to fall in place.

"Yes. I got a buddy who works downtown. He said Clay's strangled body was found behind the bus station and her friend, one of our other employees, Duane Sorensen, is missing."

"I heard the same." Carlita didn't mention the anonymous tip to the crime hotline, implicating her. "I also believe Duane Sorensen's real name is Blake Tanner."

An unreadable expression crossed Dominic's face. "He wasn't Duane Sorensen?"

"No. He was lying. Not only that, his cell phone has been disconnected, as was Monica Clay's."

"We need to do a better job of screening the applicants," Dominic said. "Or hire people with better references."

"You sound like Elvira," Carlita muttered.

"Elvira?"

"Never mind."

"So you gonna go get the applications?"

"No." Carlita's mind whirled. How much did Dominic know? Should she trust him? She slowly shook her head. "I think it's best if we wait to see how our first couple of days pan out. We might not need to hire more people."

"But I need those applications," Dominic insisted.

Carlita ignored his comment and changed the subject. "Overall, I think the guests enjoyed the wedding food, and the servers did a great job of handling the crowds. You spent most of your time in the kitchen. Did the kitchen staff complain about being overwhelmed?"

"A little." Dominic mentioned a problem with the walk-in cooler's temperature and appeared to relax as they discussed the service and the food.

They went over the work schedule for the following week, and the more Carlita thought about it, the more she was convinced they needed to stick with the employees already hired and trained.

Her cell phone chimed, and Carlita glanced at the screen. She pressed the dismiss button. "I think that about covers everything. Thank you for coming in. I'll walk you out."

Dominic followed Carlita to the front. He joined her on the sidewalk. "You sure you don't wanna bring a couple more people on board?"

"Positive." Carlita nodded firmly. "I think we'll have a better idea if or what we need after our first couple of days."

"You're the boss. I'll see you on Thursday for the all-employee meeting." Dominic waved good-bye and then crossed the street to the trolley pick up.

Carlita locked the front door before retracing her steps and making her way to the kitchen. She flipped the lights off and exited through the back door.

Back home, Carlita slipped the restaurant keys on the hook near the door and kicked off her shoes.

Mercedes popped out of her room. "Well? How did it go?"

"It was an odd meeting." Carlita sank down on the sofa. "Dominic seemed irritated when he found out I took the applications. He already knew about Monica's death and Duane Sorensen's MIA status. I was going to ask him for his thoughts on the employees, if anyone acted suspiciously, but he was acting so weird, I decided not to."

"Savannah is a small town." Mercedes flopped down on the chair. "I'm not surprised he heard about the death and the missing employee. Plus, he knew them."

Carlita frowned. "No, he didn't know them."

"Yes, he did," Mercedes said.

"He told me he didn't know them. We both agreed we needed to do a better job of screening our employees."

"He's lying." Mercedes marched to her mother's desk. She returned with the employee file folders. "Check it out."

She sifted through the applications and handed one to her mother. "This is Monica Clay's application."

Carlita's eyes narrowed as she tried to read the small print. "What am I looking for?"

"It's on the other side."

"Okay." Carlita flipped the application over. She shook her head. "I give up."

"Down there." Mercedes pointed to the bottom of the application. "Look right above the signature."

"I don't..." Carlita sucked in a breath. "What in the world?"

Chapter 24

"Monica Clay listed Dominic as a reference. He said he didn't know her. Why did he lie?" Carlita asked.

"That's not all." Mercedes pulled out another application and handed it to her mother. "Duane Sorensen also listed Dominic as a reference."

Carlita stared at the application in disbelief. "No wonder he was desperate to get his hands on the applications."

She tossed the application on top of the folder and stood. "I want to ask him to his face why he lied to me. I bet we can still catch him. He was at the trolley stop across the street a few minutes ago."

She flung the front door open and marched down the steps.

"No!" Mercedes ran after her mother. "You don't want to confront him."

"Why not?"

"Because there's a reason he lied to you. Maybe he was behind Megan Burelli's poisoning. Think about it. If he was involved and you confront him, he's going to lie or worse."

"He'll come after us," Carlita whispered.

"What if Louie hired him?"

"Then we're all in danger."

"Right."

"If we don't confront him, how do we find out if he's involved?"

"We set a trap," Mercedes said. "If Dominic is involved, we know he's desperate to get his hands on the applications. He must know or at least suspect Monica and Duane used him as a reference."

"So how do we set a trap?"

299

"Dominic has a key to the restaurant," Mercedes said.

"Yes, and now I'm wondering how I'm gonna get it back from him."

"You're not. This is perfect." Mercedes told her mother they needed to make copies of the applications and then put the originals back in the restaurant's filing cabinet. "You call Dominic and tell him you changed your mind. After talking to me, you decided to hire a few more people, and you put the applications back inside the restaurant."

"So he'll come after them," Carlita said.

"Yep, and we're going to let him take the applications. Ten bucks says he's going to alter the applications and take his name off as a reference."

"So what? It's not illegal. Troubling? Yes. Illegal? No."

"True, but if he's working with someone else, don't you think he'll go for the applications and then take them to his accomplice to get rid of them?"

Mercedes asked. "We have a 50/50 chance of someone else being involved."

"And it won't hurt to see what he does once he gets his hands on the applications," Carlita said. "Dominic uses the trolley to get around and guess who's working today?"

"Reese," Carlita and Mercedes said in unison.

"Let's get this sting underway."

While Mercedes made copies of the applications, Carlita texted Reese and asked her to call as soon as possible. Thankfully, Reese called a short time later.

Carlita briefly explained what happened, how she thought her restaurant manager was somehow involved in Megan Burelli and Monica Clay's deaths, maybe even Duane Sorensen's disappearance.

"Oh, I know Dominic. He was just on the trolley. He got off near the City Market. Nice guy. Kind of a braggart, but entertaining."

"We're setting up a sting. If our hunch is right, he'll come back down here to grab the applications. Once he does, we need to follow him, to find out where he goes."

"He typically gets off on the other side of Walton Square. It always struck me as odd why he wouldn't walk a few blocks, but hey, who am I to question strange behavior?"

"Would you do me a huge favor and send me a text if he gets back on the trolley?" Carlita asked.

"You betcha. I'm circling around to his pickup area in a couple more stops."

"Let me text him now."

Mercedes ran next door to return the applications to the cabinet. Meanwhile, Carlita texted Dominic to tell him she was having second thoughts and would consider hiring more people. In her last sentence, she told him she'd returned the applications to the restaurant filing cabinet.

A breathless Mercedes flew inside the apartment. "The applications are in place. Did you call Dominic?"

"I sent a text. I wasn't sure I would sound believable." Carlita's phone beeped, and she gazed at the screen. "He said he would get right on it. We better be ready to move. I want to see where he goes once he grabs the files."

"We can hide behind the dumpster," Mercedes suggested.

"What if he uses the front door?"

"I doubt it. He's gonna want to keep a low profile." Mercedes paused. "No. You're right. We need to cover all of our bases. You hide behind the dumpster. There's an old fence in that vacant lot across the street. I'll hide behind the fence."

With a plan in place, the women hurried to get into position. Mercedes disappeared around the corner, and Carlita got comfortable behind the dumpster.

She crouched low, keeping one eye on her cell phone, waiting for Reese's text and the other on the back door of the restaurant. She eased into a low stretch when she caught a movement out of the corner of her eye.

It was Dominic, making a beeline for the back door. Carlita ducked down and peeked around the corner. She watched him unlock the back door and slip inside.

Finally, Reese's text came through. "He's here. I'm holding the trolley for a few. He said he'd be right back."

"Thanks, Reese."

Carlita forced herself to remain calm as she kept a close eye on the back door, waiting for Dominic to emerge.

He exited the building moments later. Tucked under his arm were several manila folders.

The restaurant manager glanced around, pausing briefly when his eyes fell on the dumpster. Carlita squeezed her eyes shut; certain he knew she was back there and watching him.

She didn't let out the breath she was holding until he jogged around the corner and disappeared from sight.

Carlita stayed put until Mercedes appeared. "Did you see him?"

"Yep. He took the folders."

"He got back on the trolley," Mercedes said. "Reese waited for him."

"Now all we have to do is wait for Reese to tell us where he was going."

*****

Reese impatiently tapped the trolley steering wheel. "You better hurry up, dude. I can't wait here all day." It wasn't necessarily against company policy to hold the trolley and wait for someone.

It also wasn't necessarily an approved practice. She stared at the side of Ravello's Ristorante and willed Dominic to emerge. Thankfully, he appeared a short time later, in a hurry and carrying file folders, just as Carlita suspected.

"Thanks for waiting, Reese. You're a doll." Dominic moved to the center of the bus.

"You're welcome." She pulled the trolley onto the street and drove to the next stop.

Two passengers exited while another got on. She greeted the woman by name and then waited until the new passenger found an empty seat before resuming her route.

At the next stop, another passenger got off. The only riders left on the trolley were a small group of tourists, Dominic and Reese.

Up next was the stop where Dominic typically exited the trolley. He hurried down the center aisle. In his haste, he knocked one of the file folders from his grasp.

The papers dumped onto the floor, and he scrambled to pick them up.

"Take your time," Reese said. "I'm not in a hurry."

"What a klutz." Dominic shoved the papers back inside the folder and made his way to the front.

"We'll see you later, Dominic."

"See you later, Reese. Thanks again for waiting for me." Dominic bounded down the steps and looked both ways before crossing the street.

Reese started to ease her foot off the brake when something told her to wait. She watched Carlita's restaurant manager stroll down the sidewalk. He stopped in front of a local restaurant, smoothed his hair and then disappeared inside.

*****

Carlita and her daughter waited for several long, agonizing minutes. She glanced at her phone every few seconds, willing it to ring. "I think Reese forgot about us."

"She didn't forget," Mercedes said. "We need to be patient."

Finally, Carlita's cell phone chimed. Her eyes widened as she read Reese's text. "You're never gonna believe where Dominic went."

"To the police station," Mercedes guessed.

"No. I wish. Reese said he appeared very nervous. He got off three stops up. She waited to see where he went. He went into Russo Brother's Italian Eatery, and he was carrying our employee applications."

"What does that mean?"

"I...don't know. All this time, I figured Louie was behind the food poisoning. What if it wasn't Louie?" Carlita asked. "What if it was a supposed friend...another restaurant owner in the neighborhood trying to sabotage my new restaurant?"

"Mike Russo? He seems like a nice man," Mercedes said.

"Those are the ones you gotta watch out for. Dominic is there now."

"It's only a coupla blocks away," Mercedes said. "I say we head over there and see if we can figure out what's going on."

"Are you saying we should confront him? What if he's the one who poisoned Megan Burelli and murdered Monica Clay?"

"We'll play it by ear." Mercedes patted her pocket. "I'm packing heat, just in case. The sooner we get to the bottom of this, the better."

It was a brisk dash to the other end of Walton Square. By the time they reached Russo's restaurant, Carlita was out of breath. "We need to stay out of sight."

She glanced down the sidewalk, to a narrow alley behind the building. "This must be where Reese dropped Dominic off."

"We can watch from over there." Mercedes motioned to a box truck, parked off to the side.

"I can't believe this." Carlita crept in next to her daughter. "Pete told me Russo was expanding his operations and adding catering. Who would stoop so low as to kill a competitor's guest just to put them out of business?"

"We don't know that for sure," Mercedes warned. "It could be Dominic working on his own."

"No. Something fishy is going on." The restaurant's screen door slowly opened. An employee emerged. The smell of cigarette smoke wafted in the air.

Carlita leaned against the box truck and closed her eyes, an image of Megan Burelli filling her mind. She should've known Louie's MO wouldn't be to sneak around trying to poison Vinnie and Brittney.

The "family's" style was more like drive-by shooters. They wouldn't bother to call a crime hotline to implicate Carlita as Monica Clay's killer.

They also wouldn't have a reason to kill her, unless of course, she'd been hired as a hit woman.

The fact Pete found her crying in the alley was suspect. Had she been in on the plot to poison wedding guests, realized the seriousness of the situation, had a sudden change of heart and refused to finish the job?

Mercedes nudged her mother's arm and motioned toward the building.

Carlita dropped to her hands and knees and peered under the frame of the truck. She could see Dominic standing with his back to her and facing another unknown figure. He stood close to the other person, and she could hear them talking in low voices.

The brief conversation ended. Dominic turned on his heel and began walking at a fast clip.

With Dominic out of the picture, Carlita could clearly see Mike Russo. He watched Dominic for a moment before stepping back inside.

The screen door slammed shut.

"Let's go." Mercedes took off after Dominic, leaving her mother behind.

Chapter 25

Carlita hurried after her daughter. By the time she reached the corner, she'd lost sight of Mercedes and Dominic.

She heard loud voices coming from nearby. One of the voices belonged to Mercedes.

"Where is it?"

"I don't know what you're talking about," Dominic said. "Why are you following me?"

"Hello."

Her manager's jaw dropped when Carlita joined them. "What's going on?"

"What did you do with the employee file folders?" Carlita pointed at Dominic's empty hands. "Did you give them to Mike Russo?"

"You two are crazy. I think it's time for you to look for another restaurant manager."

"I was thinking the same thing," Carlita shot back. "In fact, I was thinking the police will be interested in the fact you gave my employee folders to my competitor, a man I thought was my friend, Mike Russo."

"That's absurd. I don't know Russo."

"You're lying." Mercedes waved her cell phone in the air. "I have proof you left the restaurant with our employee file folders, yet you didn't have them when you were in the alley behind the restaurant talking to Russo."

Dominic's countenance changed in an instant and a menacing sneer marred his face. "So what if I took the file folders? Maybe I lost 'em."

"Inside Russo's restaurant?" Mercedes shook her head. "I don't think so. I think you ditched the employee applications for other reasons. You lied

314

about knowing Monica Clay and Duane Sorensen, and now you're lying about the applications."

"Those two employees listed you as a reference, yet you claim you didn't know them," Carlita said. "Again, I'm sure the authorities will be interested in talking to you."

"It's your word against mine," Dominic jeered. "Prove it."

"We will when we give the authorities copies of the applications, the ones we made before we set the trap and waited for you to come after them. We have proof you knew the victims," Carlita said. "You came highly recommended by Mike Russo, President of the Savannah Area Restaurant Association. You were a plant."

Dominic's expression turned from a sneer to a look of fear. "You're messing with the wrong people."

"Mike Russo?" Carlita switched tactics. "Maybe if you tell the authorities everything you know, they'll go easy on you."

Dominic lunged forward. Things moved fast as Mercedes yanked her gun out of her pocket and aimed it at him. "Back off!"

"Whoa." The man lifted both hands. "You two are looney tunes. I think you killed your own wedding guest, you killed Monica Clay, and you also killed Duane Sorensen."

"Sorensen is still alive," Carlita said. "He's also ready to talk."

Dominic's mouth dropped open. "He's still alive?"

"Yes," Carlita fibbed. "He's ready to tell the authorities exactly what happened the day of the wedding, how you and he, along with Monica Clay, were hired by Mike Russo to poison my guests and ruin my business."

316

"Everything was going as planned until Monica Clay freaked out," Mercedes said. "You all thought she was going to talk. Duane knew they were in trouble and you were coming after them, so they bought bus tickets and planned to leave town."

"Y-you."

Carlita could see Dominic was at a loss for words. She had no proof Russo was involved. She did suspect Dominic. He was working in the kitchen around the time Megan was served what she now suspected was poisoned food.

"No wonder you came so highly recommended by Mike Russo. It was a setup. You and Mike planned to take out several of my guests," Carlita guessed. "Megan's tray was full of tainted food, but she panicked and only served it to one person."

She continued. "You got to Monica and took her out, but somehow, Duane slipped through your fingers. I'm sure you have people out there trying to hunt him down right now. I also bet you're the one who placed an anonymous call to the crime hotline, telling the authorities I was responsible for Megan Burelli and Monica Clay's deaths."

"The cops will never find me." Dominic stumbled back and then took off running.

Mercedes started to pursue, but Carlita stopped her. "Let him go. We need to get to the police station as soon as possible. If Duane Sorensen is alive, the police need to find him, and fast."

"What do you think Russo will do to Dominic?"

"I don't know," Carlita shuddered. "If all of our hunches are correct, he's responsible. But why kill innocent people?"

"Because you were muscling in on Russo's territory. My theory is he felt threatened and saw a perfect opportunity to poison your guests, hoping it would run you out of business before you ever opened your doors. Dominic was his man."

"I guess for some people money trumps everything." Carlita reached for her daughter's arm.

"C'mon. Let's go home. We'll grab our copies of the applications and then head to the police station."

"We should turn in the leftover appetizers, too."

"Good idea." Carlita pointed at Mercedes' gun. "But first, can you please put that thing away? You make me nervous."

*****

Neither Officer Clousen nor Detective Polivich was at the precinct. After explaining to the desk clerk that they possessed potential evidence in the Monica Clay murder investigation, the clerk radioed the officer and the detective.

Half an hour later, Detective Polivich arrived and Clousen a short time later. They ushered mother and daughter into a back room where they took turns laying out their theory and handing off the evidence, including the leftover appetizers from the wedding reception.

"This is an interesting turn of events." Detective Polivich perused Monica Clay's application before placing it on top of the pile. "You're saying your restaurant manager, Dominic Guzman, may also be the anonymous crime hotline tipster? He was working for the owner of Russo's Italian Eatery, to murder one or more of your wedding guests."

"Yes," Carlita nodded. "I believe that's the case. They killed Monica Clay after she panicked and tried to leave town with Duane Sorensen aka Blake Taylor. I'm sure you know by now which is his real name."

"We believe Sorensen is still alive," Mercedes said. "We fibbed and told Dominic Guzman that Duane contacted us, and he freaked out."

"Let me put out a couple of APBs. I'll see if we can't step up the search for Sorensen aka Taylor and also try to track down Dominic Guzman before he skips town." Officer Clousen stepped out of the office.

"What about Mike Russo?" Carlita turned to Polivich. "He's definitely a suspect."

"We need more evidence and a chance to talk to Guzman first," Detective Polivich said. "Russo has connections in town. He sits on the restaurant board. We'll have to proceed carefully."

The detective stood - his signal the meeting had ended. "In the meantime, you may want to watch your backs, if what you're telling us is true." He escorted them to the lobby. "We'll be in touch as soon as we follow up on your information."

During the walk home, Carlita mulled over the turn of events. It all started when Duane Sorensen left the headless cake topper on their back steps. Little did he know Elvira's camera was recording his every move.

Carlita suspected Sorensen might have also been the one who broke into the restaurant. Next was Megan's poisoning. Monica realized she'd injured the woman, freaked out and abandoned the plan.

Duane, now identified as Blake, may have had second thoughts, as well, or maybe he was the one who murdered Monica, convinced she was going to talk.

Dominic must have suspected, or maybe he knew he was listed as a reference on the employee applications. Carlita had trusted him implicitly, given the glowing recommendation from Mike Russo. She only briefly glanced at the applications. The fact he denied it and lied was the first clue.

"I was certain Vito's nemesis, Louie, from the family was responsible for Megan's death. All the while, it was a trusted employee. I am a terrible judge of character," Carlita lamented.

"Maybe you should put me in charge of hiring the restaurant employees, too," Mercedes teased.

"I suck at being a business owner."

"No, you don't, Ma. You're a savvy entrepreneur, not to mention a great role model."

"Thanks, Mercedes. Sometimes, I do wonder." Carlita changed the subject. "When we get home, we need to get ready for dinner. I'm starving."

"Wait 'til we tell Tony and Paulie what happened," Mercedes said. "They're not going to believe it."

"I'm having a hard time believing it myself."

Chapter 26

Carlita nervously clasped her hands. "I don't know if I'm ready for this."

"You're as ready as you're ever going to be." Pirate Pete patted her shoulder. "This is the fun stuff, the real test of your willpower and grit."

"Thanks for being here, for pitching in these last few days, not to mention loaning me one of your restaurant managers after Dominic's arrest."

Pirate Pete shook his head. "I was shocked when I found out the authorities arrested Mike Russo and charged him, along with Dominic, with the murders of Megan Burelli and Monica Clay. Did you hear back on the appetizers you turned in to the authorities...if they contained traces of poison?"

"They were clean. My guess is Monica tossed the tainted stuff in the dumpster after taking the tray away, which could be around the time you saw Blake and Monica in the alley. Why she picked Megan as her target...we may never know."

Carlita continued. "Dominic and Russo might've gotten away with it if the police hadn't finally caught up with Blake Taylor over on Tybee Island. He confessed to his part in Megan's death, how Russo paid all three of them."

She tapped the tip of her chin thoughtfully. "What do you think will happen to Russo's restaurant?"

"I heard his brother, Pietro, is going to run it."

Carlita could see several people milling about out front, waiting to be among the first to dine at Ravello's Ristorante. "It's now or never." She signaled for the server to open the doors.

Pete smiled. "I was thinking with Russo in jail...there's an opening for the president of the Savannah Area Restaurant Association. You should apply."

Carlita's eyes widened in horror. "No way. Can you picture me heading up a committee of all of the restaurant owners in the Savannah area?"

"Yes." A slow smile spread across Pete's face. "I can picture you handling that amongst other things."

He nodded toward the entrance, where a group of hungry diners gathered, waiting to be seated. "Ravello's Ristorante is finally, officially open for business."

The end.

If you enjoyed reading "Matrimony & Mayhem," please take a moment to leave a review. It would be greatly appreciated. Thank you.

The series continues...book 12 in the "Made in Savannah Cozy Mystery" series coming soon!

Books in This Series

Made in Savannah Cozy Mystery Series

Meet the Author

Hope loves to connect with her readers! Connect with her today!

Never miss another book deal! Text the word Books to 33222

Visit **hopecallaghan.com/newsletter** for special offers, free books,
and soon-to-be-released books!

**Pinterest:
https://www.pinterest.com/cozymysteriesau thor/**

**Facebook:
https://www.facebook.com/authorhopecalla ghan/**

Hope Callaghan is an author who loves to write Christian books, especially Christian Mystery and Cozy Mystery books. She has written more than 50 mystery books (and counting) in five series.

In March 2017, Hope won a Mom's Choice Award for her book, "Key to Savannah," Book 1 in the Made in Savannah Cozy Mystery Series.

Born and raised in a small town in West Michigan, she now lives in Florida with her husband.

She is the proud mother of one daughter and a stepdaughter and stepson. When she's not doing the thing she loves best - writing books - she enjoys cooking, traveling and reading books.

Garlucci Italian Cookie Recipe

Ingredients:

1 cup butter, softened
2 cups sugar
3 large eggs
1 – 15 oz. container ricotta cheese
2 teaspoons vanilla extract
4 cups all-purpose flour
1 teaspoon salt
1 teaspoon baking soda

(Frosting):

1/4 cup butter, softened
3 to 4 cups confectioners' sugar
1/2 teaspoon vanilla extract
3 to 4 tablespoons milk
3 tablespoons cream cheese, softened
½ teaspoon lemon zest (optional)

Directions:

-Preheat oven to 350 degrees.
- Combine flour, salt and baking soda in medium bowl. Set aside.
- In large bowl, cream butter and sugar.
-Add eggs one at a time. Beat well after adding each one.
-Add ricotta cheese and vanilla.

330

-Mix thoroughly.
- Slowly add dry mixture to sugar mixture.
-Mix thoroughly.

-Drop by rounded teaspoonful, roughly two inches apart onto greased baking sheets.
-Bake at 350° for 10-12 minutes or until lightly browned.
-Remove and set aside to cool.

-While cookies cool, cream butter, confectioners' sugar, vanilla, cream cheese and lemon zest.
-Add a tablespoon of milk, one at a time until frosting is smooth.
-Frost cooled cookies.
-Store in the refrigerator.